THE GAME

DON McLEAN

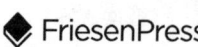 FriesenPress

Suite 300 - 990 Fort St
Victoria, BC, V8V 3K2
Canada

www.friesenpress.com

Copyright © 2019 by Don McLean
First Edition — 2019

All rights reserved.

No part of this publication may be reproduced in any form, or by any means, electronic or mechanical, including photocopying, recording, or any information browsing, storage, or retrieval system, without permission in writing from FriesenPress.

ISBN
978-1-5255-3335-8 (Hardcover)
978-1-5255-3336-5 (Paperback)
978-1-5255-3337-2 (eBook)

1. Fiction, Mystery & Detective

Distributed to the trade by The Ingram Book Company

I want to thank my friend, and wife Lori for all your inspiration. You were the one by my side all these years, you were the one who pushed me to write my stories down. For that I am grateful. All my Love.

NIGHT ONE

"I know I'm new to this, but can I try playing the game?" Barry asked, like a small child with a secret. "I think I know how to kill someone."

"Sure." Franco gestured with his hand as a maitre d' would when allowing someone to pass. "Remember the rules?"

"Yeah sure. I can make up a story about the victim, mostly so we learn to hate him. Then I can describe a scenario around his death. Oh yeah, I can only use things in a hospital to kill him. Okay, here goes." Barry leaned forward.

"Night shifts are eerie at times—lights off, shadows, no one walking the halls like they do during the day shift. Walking the halls of a hospital at night reminds me of so many horror movies. The walls seem to hold their own shadows of patients long gone. That's when I do my best work. So that's why it's so easy for me to walk into a room and do my business. This night, I decide to pick this particular patient. He is forever bitching and complaining, and he treats the staff like crap. He is about fifty-six-years old and runs a large financial firm. But he likes to overcharge good people who are trying to save for retirement. He has his minions running from early morning to late at night. The more clients, the more commission. Edwards has no time for slackers. "If you're not working the business, you're not making the commission" – that's his motto. He insists that clients are idiots, and only he knows what people need. This morning, Edwards woke up and felt left-arm pains radiating into his chest. Edwards blew it off as stiffness until he arrived at the office, where his secretary saw him sweating and a little short of breath. Like most guys when they're in pain or have a cold, theirs is the worst, no one has ever had this type of pain, and so on."

"Get to the point, Barry." Franco was already bored.

"So, Edwards begged his long-time secretary to call 911. EMS arrived at the office to take him to the hospital. Mr. Edwards was admitted for an inferior myocardial infarction. That's a heart attack on the right side of the heart. It took less than thirty minutes to get the slightly overweight, slightly gray-haired man from his office to the emergency department and to the Cardiac Cath lab where they opened the right coronary artery (RCA) that supplied the fat-surrounded heart of Mr. Edwards. The cardiologist wanted to keep the arterial line in for a few hours prior to pulling it to ensure the artery didn't close up. Edwards is on the CSU unit. All his vital signs are stable. He is on telemetry to watch for arrhythmias while he's in the step-down unit. The good news is, he is down in the middle of the unit, so no one will notice me going into the room. The step-down unit is one large hallway with about sixteen rooms, most of them with double beds that are separated only by a curtain. The rooms are dark and could use a paint job that suits this decade. Edwards is in the bed by the door, which is always partially open. I take a small syringe with about 1 cc or so of air and inject it into the arterial line. The air bubble travels up to the heart, and bang. He has instant chest pain and runs of ventricular tachycardia. By then, I had slipped into the next room while everyone ran to his bedside."

"Wait a minute, I've seen air bubbles go through a coronary artery. It hurts like shit but will pass. The code team would give nitro and probably get him back to the Cardiac Cath lab. I call bullshit, Barry that will never kill someone." Franco pointed to Barry in a way that indicated; don't pull that shit with me. "That's bullshit!" Franco still shaking his head in disapproval.

"Okay, let's wrap this up and check our patients." Katlin pushed her chair back as she moved to her room.

"Yes, boss," Franco replied, just as if his mother had told him to go do his homework.

The CCU team all rise to check in on their patients. We usually do this every couple of hours, more if a patient is critical. Tonight, all was well for some of us.

"Hi, Mrs. Johnson. How are you feeling tonight?" Bev called as she pushed herself out of the chair and strolled into her room.

"Oh, I feel good, I'm just waiting for my friend to come pick me up." Mrs. Johnson replied with her biggest smile, as if she knew something Bev didn't.

"It's getting late. Are you sure someone's coming, Mrs. Johnson?"

"Oh yes, he is coming to take me away." Violet Johnson is in our unit, waiting to be placed in a care home. She had an abdominal aortic aneurysm repair and will just not be able to manage her activities of daily living. Violet's daughters tell us that she once was quite the looker and loved to flirt with the boys. A regular Betty Boop.

"Mrs. Johnson, I think you may be mixed-up." Bev now realized what the situation was.

"No, I'm not, and if you don't leave my house now, I will have my boyfriend call the police on you! Why are you in my house? What is your name?"

"Oh, Mrs. Johnson, I am here to give you your medicine, as I always am. You're in the hospital, getting better. Now here, let me give you your medicine." Bev calmed Violet Johnson down.

"Oh boy, sundowner's syndrome, must be a full moon or something out there." Bev muttered to herself.

Sun downer's syndrome occurs to mostly the elderly that have been in the hospital or a retirement home. It is sometimes associated with early Alzheimer's. Nonetheless, the patient becomes confused and is just not aware of where they are. These patients just can't seem to get to sleep because their minds won't allow them to rest, which makes for long nights form both the patients and for us. Sometimes, if you have more than a couple of these patients, it's easier to put them together and let them talk to each other. Bev enjoyed taking care of all types of patients, but sometimes trying to talk to someone who loses reality as soon as the sun sets is a challenge.

"My mother was like that when she was in the hospital," Bev stated, as she walked out of the room. "She believed her boyfriend was coming to pick her up. Not only that, she also thought she was pregnant. She would watch an old-time dance band on TV; they were all gray-haired musicians. The lead singer of the band would close by saying, 'see you soon.' So, my mom thought he was talking to her." Bev told everyone her mother's story, not that anyone in particular was listening.

Report is quick, simple, and concise. The day charge person has a large master list that includes each patient and their medical problems—what they came in with as well as any complications. This master sheet provides some insight to how the patient and family are doing or progressing. The assignments are handed out according to the information on this page. Most of the time, the assignments work. But occasionally, we need to make changes because of who might be working that night, or if patients from the emergency department are sicker than expected.

"Hey guys, let's get done quickly. A friend of mine is being admitted, and I want to run down to the Emergency department (ER)." Katlin sat down to complete the first round of charting.

"Hi Mrs. Adams, how are you tonight?"

"Good, thank you, it seems my blood pressure is getting under control."

"That's good news, ma'am. I have a pill that the doctor asked me to give to you. I think it will help you sleep. Let me get you some water. I'll just get some water from the bathroom."

"Now all I have to do is make her drink this water with this whole bottle of tetrahydrozoline and she will sleep. If this works, I may have to use it a few more times." The culprit half-smiled as the eye drops swirled into the water

"Thank you, Nurse. I do need a good night's sleep."

"Yes, Mrs. Adams. This will help. Sleep tight."

CHAPTER ONE

"Hey, dad, are you coming to my game?" The young voice was hopeful. "I'm pitching tonight. Hope you can make it. See ya. Luv you."

"End of message one."

"Next Message."

Message two.

"Hi, John. I have those files you asked for. Took a little doing, but I've got them in hand. Most of the reports are redacted, but you'll get the gist of them. You should get them in a day or so. Cheers…"

"End of message two."

"Next Message."

Message three.

"Hey! Hi! This message is for John Smith. I'm not 100 percent sure of what's going on at The South Regional trauma hospital. But people are dying, and the cause seems suspicious! Catch the nurse who is doing this before it's too late. Oh yeah, this is Martha Hayward—the one who is telling you this, not the one committing the crimes. I am a nurse at SRTH. You can call me at the hospital, or my cell phone at 303 502 1124. Bye"

"End of message three."

While Mr. Smith sat in his harvest-green office, located on the upper floor of the 55th precinct, he studied his old-style answering machine for the number of his last caller. The display read 'phone number unavailable.' "Not much help there," he thought.

Mr. Smith pulled his little black book from his plaid sport coat with the brown elbow patches. The black notepad is where he keeps his notes. Like a news reporter, he begins to write a few more notes for reference later. John Smith has been on the force for more years than he cares to consider. Now, with more gray hair than black, he stands about 5 foot 9 inches. He was probably taller in his early years, but pounding the pavement as a cop and now as a detective will do that to you. Smith has a few things to wrap up prior heading out for the night. Looking at his notebook, he knows he needs to follow up with his old friend and with this person who thinks nurses are killing nurses or patients.

"Okay, Kurt, will you be so kind to watch my patients while I'm down in the ER?" Katlin spoke to him as she looked over Kurt's shoulder as he wrote his assessments.

"Sure, Katlin. Anything going on with them?" Kurt looked up at Katlin, not really expecting a report.

"No, they're all okay. Unless they want water or pain medications."

Katlin is the charge person for most nights. She has worked hard to get back to the bedside. Katlin took time off from nursing to work at an insurance company as a forensic chart investigator or auditor. Her job was to detect and report any potential fraud from hospitals, patients, and anyone else who might think about ripping off the insurance company. Katlin became very experienced and knowledgeable about the many ways a patient or hospital could bill for treatments, medication, and other tests. The more she worked with this type of material, the more intrigued she became. Now, Katlin is always thinking about what the motive is behind some charges, tests, or just inconsistencies in the charts. One of the most common problems arose when a subject had stopped a medication, but the charges for that same medication continued for a few days after the stop order was written. That might not sound like much, but the cost of medication provided to a patient is several times higher than what it would cost to purchase that same medication in a pharmacy. This could easily run into the thousands of dollars per patient before that patient is discharged.

The best part about Katlin's former job was that it could be done from home. This allowed her time with her daughter Meghan. Katlin was able to take Meghan to school or too many of Meghan's extra-curricular activities.

Katlin's true love was critical care nursing. Eventually, Katlin came back to the hospital. But administration felt she had been away too long and needed to take a refresher course. Katlin agreed to do so, and she quickly completed the required classes and now is back home in critical care.

This was the first time I met Katlin. We seemed to connect during the classroom lectures. We had coffee and drinks after class. Perhaps this is where I first became attracted to Katlin. We seemed to hit it off. Most times it was flirting.

"I brought you an apple, teacher." Katlin would give me with her usual sheepish grin.

"Thanks for your help again, Palmer. You make this transition back to the hospital much more enjoyable." She would tell me each day. Katlin is one of the most respected nurses in the hospital. Almost everyone knows her and her good cheer. All knew of her reputation as an amazing nurse and person.

Katlin rushed down to the ER, pushing through doors like she was on a mission.

"Hey, Mary, how are you? Bob called me and said you were coming in." Katlin leaned over the emergency room stretcher to give her friend a long hug.

Taking a deep breath, Mary responded, "I'm okay. I'm sure it's nothing," and she smiled up half-heartedly at Katlin.

"I felt some pains down my left arm and into my chest. But I was washing floors yesterday and was sure it's just stiffness. Anyway, Bob called 911, and here I am."

"Let me look at your chart and see what the doc has to say." Katlin picked up Mary's chart and was already into the review.

"Well, Miss Kate, what a pleasant surprise. What brings you down to our end of the hospital?" Dr. Sandoval had entered the room with his usual big smile.

"Doc, this is my best friend, Mary." Are you taking care of her, I hope?"

"Yes, ma'am." Dr. Sandoval now stood beside Katlin.

"Well, what do the labs say? What are the troponin levels? What does the ECG say?" Katlin asked, now into her detective mode.

"Slow down, Katlin. We ran all the usual tests."

"I don't see them in the chart. When were they drawn?" Katlin flipped through the chart.

"You know, I heard about your past life as a forensic auditor. Now I see why so many people love working with you. You're always looking for the answers."

"Sorry, Doc. Bad habit. I know you've done everything you can at the moment."

Dr. Sandoval looked at Mary. "Okay, Mary, we want to take you to the Cardiac Cath lab to have a look at a possible blockage of your anterior descending coronary artery. LAD for short. This is the front side of your heart."

"Does that mean it's my heart, Doctor? I mean did I really have a heart attack?"

"Yes, Mary. Moreover, it is the front part of your heart. That is a very serious area of the heart."

"Okay, Doc. Will Mary come see us in CCU, or will she go to our step-down unit?" Katlin focused on what Dr. Sandoval had just said.

"No need to put her into the big room. We'll send her to the step-down unit. She will be good there and in a couple days she should be able to go home." Dr. Sandoval reassured both Katlin and Mary.

The door to the room opened and an athletically built man entered. "Oh, Bob, this is Dr. Sandoval." Katlin gave Bob a hug, as she introduced the doctor.

"Hi, Kat, how are you? Thanks for coming down to see us." Bob tried to grin.

Bob turned to Dr. Sandoval and extended his thick ranch hand to greet the doctor.

"Hello, Bob. It's nice to meet you. Your wife will be fine. She has a blockage in her heart, and we are just ready to go to the Cardiac Cath lab." Dr. Sandoval shook Bob's hand, which felt like a vise grip around his hand.

"Can I come?"

"Yes, by all means, Bob. We have a waiting room for you. After we've done the procedure, I'll come out and discuss how things went."

"Okay, thanks, Dr. Sandoval. I'll follow." Bob held Mary's hand at the bedside.

"Give us a few minutes, and we'll be on our way." Dr. Sandoval shook Bob's hand again and placed a hand on Katlin's shoulder.

"Thanks, Doctor." Bob smiled back.

"Okay, Mary, I need to get back upstairs. Dr. Sandoval is one of our best. He'll take good care of you. I'll see you and Bob upstairs when you're all done. Bob, you have my cell number. Call for anything." Katlin smiled at both Mary and Bob.

"Thanks for being with Mary. They wouldn't let me ride with her in the ambulance. So, it was good for Mary to see a familiar face."

"My pleasure, Bob. Mary and I go way back."

"I'll say." Mary now smiled as well. Since our kids rode horses together, we've been good friends."

"Bob, do you remember that ranch? What was the name?"

"Dallas horse ranch. It was a small ranch-style riding ground, right?" A smile was coming to Bob's face more easily now.

"Yes, that was it; it was in the valley. We went there before we moved to our own acreage." Mary recalled those lean years.

The Game

"Yes, back when we could sit and watch." Katlin smiled as they reminisced about the simpler times.

"You mean talk. Not sure about you, Kate, but I think we talked more than we watched. We often had to make up stories that we saw every jump because we had talked so much."

Laughing, Katlin shook her head. "Yes, the truth comes out. See you soon, luv both of you."

Because it is after hours, the Cath lab team is called in to assist. Usually, two Cath lab technicians and a radiology technician run the equipment. One technician scrubs in with the doctor and the other runs the equipment and can log in all activities, equipment used, and medications given. This data is printed out and filed in the patient's chart for records

The Cardiac Cath lab is on the main floor, one floor up from the emergency department. You have to take the service elevator and pass through a series of large, brown, electric doors to enter the holding area of the Cath lab. The six labs are identical. Much like a typical operating room, they have sterile, white walls and imposing banks of instruments. Mary could see the three monitors as the team slid her from the warm stretcher to the cold, hard table.

"Hi, Mary. I'm John. I just arrived, so let me get things started, and I will be back to talk to you."

"Okay, thank you. Have you been working here all day?" Mary trying to keep calm.

"No, ma'am, they call us at home, and we come in."

"Oh, my! I didn't mean to get you out of the house. I am so sorry."

"No, but thank you. It's okay, Mary, it's our job to come back anytime during the night."

John connected the heart monitor to Mary, and she could see her heart rate and hear the beating of her heart.

"Can you turn the heat up, I'm very cold." Mary shivered a little from either the cold room or her nervousness.

"I'll give you a warm blanket, but it's always cold in here. We need to keep all the equipment cool." John returned with a warm blanket from the blanket warmer that was located behind the table on the back wall.

"You'll be able to see what we're doing on this monitor," as John pointed to the middle monitor.

"Oh, I'm not sure I want to see that. "Mary nervously looked up at John.

The radiology tech, Karen, slid the camera over Mary.

"Mary, this is our camera that will take pictures of your heart for Dr. Sandoval to see any blockage you may have in the coronary artery."

"Did you have to come from home as well?"

"Yes, I'm Karen. It's my pleasure to come and help out tonight. Please relax and don't worry." Karen turned her attention back to the equipment in preparation for the tests.

"Mary, you'll get a hot flash from the contrast as it goes through the blood stream. Most people say they feel like they peed a little. But don't worry, that's normal." John tried his best to relax Mary as he explained what would happen.

"Hi, Mary. I'll scrub in and be behind a mask, but please feel free to ask questions." Dr. Sandoval looked down at Mary.

"Thank you, Dr. Sandoval. Will I be asleep or wide awake?"

"You'll be awake, but John will give you a shot of midazolam, which will help you relax. If you want to sleep, that's fine. I'll explain everything after we are done."

"Thanks again, Dr. Sandoval. I trust you."

Dr. Sandoval injected some lidocaine into Mary's right groin area to numb the area. Then he made a very small incision over the femoral artery.

"Pass me the arterial catheter, John."

"Here you go, Doc. Do you want to do the left ventricular ejection first or go straight to the coronary artery?"

"Let's do the ejection fraction first. I want to see how her heart muscle is beating. I suspect it will still be strong. Pass me the J catheter."

Dr. Sandoval took the long tube, much like a thirty-nine-inch straw and slid it all the way from Mary's groin to her heart.

"Okay, Mary, here comes that hot flash that I told you about." John hit the remote button on the injector as the contrast was injected through the catheter into the left ventricle and passed through the descending aorta into the lower extremities.

"Oh, my. You're right, I feel like I just peed."

"Let's shoot the left anterior descending coronary artery. It looked like that may be the culprit."

Mary could hear the camera roll as the table moved up and down to view her heart, but this didn't seem to bother Mary; the medications were relaxing her.

"Mary, I'm going to place a stent in your artery to help keep it open. The stent is like a scaffold that will keep the artery open. This is normal." Dr. Sandoval leaned over Mary.

Liz, the second tech, opened some packages and placed the stent onto the sterile table for John and Dr. Sandoval.

"You may feel a little pressure as we inflate the balloon. The balloon pushes the stent open inside the artery." John injected a small amount of contrast through the catheter while Karen took the picture.

"Oh, that looks great. Let's remove the tubes and call the CSU for a bed. Leave the arterial line in place over night."

"Yes, Sir, Dr. Sandoval." John now cleaned up the equipment and wiped off Mary's groin area.

"Mary, you did great. It's all over; we took care of the heart blockage."

"It's done? That was fast. It didn't hurt at all."

"That's great, Mary. You will have to lie flat for several hours with this tube in your right femoral artery. But we can give you something to help you relax."

"Okay, will you let my husband know what you did?"

"Yes, I will go talk to him now."

Bob was in the waiting room. The bad thing about after hours is no one is around to talk to. Bob made some coffee from the machine in the waiting area and pulled out his phone.

"Hi, Beth, it's dad. How are you, sweetie?"

"Good dad, you sound sad, kind of quiet. What's going on?"

"Sweetie, Mom had a heart attack tonight and is in the Cardiac Cath lab now with the doctor. When they're done, the doctor will come and update me." Bob talked softly, even though no one was in the waiting room with him.

"Dad, do you need me to come down? Is anyone with you? I'll come now!" Beth's voice trembled.

The Game

"No, I've been drinking coffee and reading the material they have laying around while I'm waiting. Why don't you come tomorrow? I assume mom will be sleepy tonight."

"Okay, but I'm here if you need me. Are you sure you're okay? I can come now, or I come over to the house if you're planning to go home later."

"Thanks, baby. I'm okay and your mom is in good hands. Katlin was here before your mom went in. I see the doctor coming. Call you soon. Love you"

"I love you to. Please tell mom I'm praying for her."

"Will do."

"Bye, dad. Love you"

Dr. Sandoval walked into the waiting room and removed his mask to speak to Bob.

"Hi again, Bob. Mary did great. We opened her artery. Let me review what we did." As Dr. Sandoval continued to speak, he motioned for Bob to push over so he could sit beside him on the couch "I like to provide the details because many people have a lot of unanswered questions after a procedure. We moved Mary onto the table where the technician shaved her right groin area so we could have a clean access point. She did receive some heparin to thin her blood and some morphine and versed to relax her. I made a tiny incision into the skin and then slid a lengthy catheter up the femoral artery into the aorta and positioned it to the left anterior descending artery. We used a small amount of contrast, which is injected into the coronary artery. The contrast shows up on the monitoring screen, so we can see what the situation is. With Mary, it was clear that a blockage existed mid-way down. I slid a very small, thin wire through this *J* tube into and past the blockage. Next, I inserted the balloon, which I inflated to reopen the blocked artery and placed a stent inside the artery to support the vessel. Once the artery was open, I removed the balloon and wire and then the long *J* tube. I left the artery catheter that was placed for ease of access into the femoral artery. We'll leave the arterial catheter in place over night. Then, if anything happens, like the stent closing, we have access to get in and fix any potential problems. Usually the first twenty-four hours is the most crucial. Do you have any questions for me, Bob?"

"No! Thank-you for your help and saving my wife's life." Bob exhaled a big sigh of relief.

"No problem. We'll take her up to her room, and you can talk with her."

"Thanks again, Doctor. Thank you."

John and Liz moved Mary back to the stretcher and wheeled her past the waiting room to pick Bob up.

"Hi, honey. How are you? Dr. Sandoval explained the procedure and said it went well." Bob grabbed for Mary's small hand.

"I feel so much better, no elephant on my chest anymore."

"Bob come with us, we will take you and Mary up to CSU." John positioned himself at the head of the stretcher and Bob walked along at the side of the stretcher.

In no time at all, Mary and Bob turned the corner and headed to Mary's new room.

"Hi, Mary. I'm Sandra. I'll take care of you tonight. Welcome to CSU, you're in room 23 A."

"Hi, Sandra. Can my husband come in?"

"Sure. Let's get you comfortable in bed, then your husband can come in." Sandra grabbed the curtains and started to pull them around Mary's bed for privacy.

"I'll wait here for you, dear."

"Okay, Bob. Did you call, Beth?"

"Yes, maybe now is a good time to call her back. I told her I would call her back and let her know you're well."

"You can use the phone at the desk to make calls." Sandra pointed to the main desk.

"Thanks. I'll be right back, dear."

John, Liz, and Sandra slid Mary off the stretcher onto a much more comfortable bed.

"Oh, that feels so much better. Thanks to you all." Mary was more relaxed now.

"Sandra, let me give you a report. Things went well."

"Thanks, John. Let's go out to the desk."

Bob walked over to the Nurse's station with a little more purpose in his step. The phone was on the corner of the desk, which was high enough to lean on. It occurred to him that the design probably helped when it came to writing reports or doctor orders in charts.

"Hi, Beth. It's dad. Mom is up on the floor and doing well. The procedure went well, and now she'll get some rest."

"Oh, dad, that's such great news! Say hi and I'm thinking of her. I'll be up in the morning."

"Okay, I'm going to see mom and maybe go home if all is okay."

"Okay, are you sure you don't need me to come by, dad?"

"No, we're both fine. Thanks, Beth."

"Okay, bye dad. I love you."

"Bye, sweetie. Love you too."

Bob walked back into the dark and dreary room that was supposed to relax patients and make them feel at home.

"Hi, Bob. Did you talk to Beth? Is she okay?"

"Yes, she sends her love."

"I guess I'm stuck in this dreary room for a few days. I thought this hospital would be a little more up to date with the paint and all." Mary surveyed her room.

"Yeah, it does look a little outdated with the yellowish walls and peeling wallpaper." Bob completed his survey of the room and surroundings as well.

"Remember that apartment we lived in way back when we were first married? That was a step up from this room." Bob laughed as he held Mary's hand.

"Yeah, I think they need to spend some money on renovations. Bob, you should go home and rest. I feel good, and I'm ready for a good sleep."

"Are you sure, Mary? I can stay."

"No, I'm good. Go and get a good night's sleep. Bob, I'm much better."

"I love you, dear. Have them call me for any reason at all."

"Okay, I love you to."

Bob headed out of the room and down the hall, still surveying the serious need for upgrades everywhere he looks.

The hospital has been around for years. Administration has plans for a total renovation. Bob and Mary are not the first to notice the aging walls.

Bob turned the first corner and read a sign. "CCU" with an arrow pointing up, and "SICU" with an arrow pointing in the same direction as he is headed. CCU and Surgical

Intensive Care Unit (SICU) are cornerstones of the seventh floor. Each unit has a step-down floor. CCU has CSU and SICU has SCU. The floor is joined by two long corridors on either side of the elevators. Like a big H. CSU and SCU are the legs of the H. Private and semi-private rooms are on either side of the hall, which is identical to the other unit. Mary is in one of the rooms in the middle of the unit.

"Thanks, Kurt, for looking at my patients. Hey team, can we have a quick report on all your patients?" Katlin was back on the unit.

"Man! I'll be so glad when this hospital renovates this dump. This report room is not even big enough for five people, let alone families who need somewhere to cry in privacy. I may just move one day!" Franco stated the obvious to no one in particular.

"Oh, come on, Franco. It's cozy." Bev slid the old wooden chair closer to Franco.

The team provided quick updates on the patients. Usually, the report is short and to the point. The patient faces may change, but the conditions, the heart attacks, strokes trauma all seem to remain the same. So many times, we hear; "One heart attack is the same as the other." The experience of our team is undeniable. We have all seen it, been there, and done that.

"My patient had an angioplasty and will leave tomorrow." Palmer sipped on his coffee.

"Yeah, my patient had a CABG and is an overflow from SICU. He'll go to the step-down unit in the morning." Franco jumped in.

"My girl is okay; nothing to report so far." Bev added her two cents.

"Kurt, anything to report?"

"Nope, Katlin, all is well."

"Okay, boys and girls, go forth and save lives," Katlin directed. She has a particular way of saying, go assess your patents. Tonight, the assignments worked out. We usually take what is given to us. It's not fair to request the best cases every night.

The police had been called into the hospital by the coroner's office prior to Martha's call as a matter of record. Dr. Brooks, the coroner, first notified his long-time friend at the police department when three patients, each with an unknown cause of death, came to his attention. Detective Smith was just the next man up, but he was happy to hear from his old friend. Smith was not that old, only mid-forties. But he had an old soul, dressed like an older person, and used his old-school tools and know-how. The job had made him slightly gray. Smith walked into the morgue to visit his friend.

The morgue is a large, stainless-steel-looking room. Everything is stainless steel. The front section of the room has three long tables with a type of shower hose at the head. Over the tables, lights like you see in an operating room. The back area along the wall is a set of doors. Each three-foot by three-foot door opens and a sliding table can be pulled out to view bodies or to make it easy to load and unload the bodies that eventually go the funeral homes.

Brooks and Smith didn't really grow up together; however, their careers grew up together. Brooks was a surgeon at the local hospital where Smith, as a young cop, was carried into one night. Smith had been shot in the shoulder by some gangbangers when he pulling them over for a routine check. Brooks took the bullet out and patched Smith up. Since then their paths crossed several times until they started to meet up for drinks, meals, BBQs, and the like. Brooks was a new medical examiner when one dark night Smith's wife showed up on his table. Mrs. Smith had been found on a roadside, naked and with multiple stab wounds. There have been no arrests. Neither talk much about it; it happened years ago, and it's just something that no longer needs to be talked about.

"There ain't no reason in my professional opinion that these three should have bought the farm." Dr. Brooks started in without even greeting Smith. Brooks always reminded Smith of the old doc from Gunsmoke, which he had loved in his earlier days. Brooks is a short, stout, gray-haired man who has seen a thing or two in the past. People tend to dismiss Brooks because of his age or his small-town act. But, in fact, he's one of the most respected surgeons and pathologist in the region. "Do you ever stop taking notes?" Brooks looked over Smith's shoulder as Smith continued to write. "I believe this might be the work of a health care professional, like a nurse or doctor." Brooks continued.

"Why do you say that?" Smith looked up from his notes.

"Well, if it was a civilian, there would be marks or scars, or the tox screens would be positive. But I ain't seen nothing like that. Not many civilians would know how to kill someone, let alone sneak into a hospital and off someone."

"They seem random," replied Smith, while adding more notes to his book.

"Random! What makes you think these are random? Each of these patients have either money, influence, or connections to the administration. Someone has been thinking, planning these deaths," Brooks continued.

"This is a sixty-five-year old man, Jack M. Fletcher." Brooks looked at a chart. "Died of a heart attack"

"What's suspicious" about that?" Smith looked at the chart with Brooks.

"Well, you usually have blocked arteries. This guy didn't. I suspect he could've been given a large dose of potassium. That will cause death."

"Okay, how many of these deaths do you have?"

"Three that don't add up." Brooks tossed his chart on the desk.

Smith closed his book. "Thanks, Doc. I'll stay in touch. I have to run, got a baseball game to get to. And thanks for the call, Doc. As always, it's good to see you again, even if it is under these circumstances."

"John, before you go, I heard about this woman up on the floors the other day. She didn't die, but she came close."

"So how does that involve me, Doc?"

"Well, no direct reason. The patient told her nurse that another nurse came in and gave her a pill to help her sleep. The first nurse said there was no other nurse that would have given her a sleeping pill. Then, out of nowhere, the patient started to have diarrhea, headaches, flushing. All that fun stuff."

"Wow, quite the story, Doc. Thanks." Mr. Smith impatiently headed to the door.

"No, wait. The pill was just a Tylenol, but the lady's eye drop medication was empty. I think whoever did this to these patients may have practised on this lady. She used tetrahydrozoline, which, if you watch TV, know that characters use it to try killing people. I heard about this a few weeks ago and didn't think much of it. But it looks like, if there is a killer, he or she is getting better at disguising it."

"So, other than an empty bottle, what makes you think it was intentional?" Smith was back in his book jotting some notes down.

"We used LC-MS/MS, which is a test performed in 80% of case reports like this. It's the best way to detect tetrahydrozoline."

"LCM, what?" Smith added some more scratches to his book.

"Liquid chromatography, tandem mass spectrometry, John."

"Okay, thanks for that. That's interesting." John pushed on the door.

"Okay. Say hi to Jordan for me, will ya?"

"Will do, Brooks. Take care."

Smith's son Jordon is almost thirteen-years old and has been playing baseball since he was about five. All he wants to do is pitch. His goal is to pitch for the San Francisco Giants. Tonight, Jordan is pitching against the rival team. Jordan got a ride from one of the moms, and Smith arrived in time to watch most of the game. Tonight is no different from other nights. It's the middle of the second inning, and

Jordan is ready to go back to the mound. Jordan's team, the White Sox, are up three to one.

"Hi, John. You should've seen Jordan pitch. He struck out two and flied out one."

"Hi, Lynn. Thanks for picking him up. Yeah, he is quite the pitcher." Smith settled onto the bleacher next to Lynn, a single mom who plays mom and dad for her son.

"The coach wants him to pitch the first four innings, at least that is what I heard the coach tell Jordan." Lynn continued.

"Yeah, he mentioned this to Jordan last game. Since then, Jordan has been in the backyard every evening, working on his fastball and changeup."

"Oh, you must be so proud, John."

"Yes, I am. But you should be to. Matte has been on fire with his bat. He'll go a long way with his bat and fielding skills."

"Yeah, I take him to every camp there is out there. Costs a fortune."

"Jordan's the same. He's had a pitching coach for the last five years."

"Let's go, buddy, 1-2-3, find your corners bud!" Get Smith around baseball, and he can't hold back, hollering out to the mound.

Jordan's teammates are doing the usual chanting. "Hey batter, batter, batter! Swing batter, swing batter."

"Wow, he's throwing well. Lynn also clapping at each pitch. He's struck out two more."

"Yeah, those coaching sessions are really doing Jordy good. His mechanics have improved over the winter. His coach said he's topping out at 85 MPH."

The Game

"John, that's amazing! How long has he been with his coach?"

"We started two winters ago. He does all kinds of pre-pitching drills and routines. It's really a science now." John half watched the game and glanced at Lynn.

"Maybe I need to take Matte to a coach to fine-tune his skills."

"Oh yeah, for sure, Lynn. Ben has helped many kids with batting, fielding skills, and pitching. Here's his card."

"Thanks, John. I'll check it out."

The rest of the game went well. Jordan pitched a five hitter and allows only three runs. The Sox had nine hits and scored six runs.

"Great job, Jordy, you played well." Smith gave the usual high five to Jordan.

"Thanks, dad. Thanks for coming out. I know you're busy."

"Matte, you hit some bombs today. Great job, kiddo."

"Thanks, Mr. Smith. I missed a couple, but it was fun."

"Oh, Matte, I am so proud of you. You were amazing."

"Thanks, Mom, I felt good today."

"Well, do you two rock stars want pizza, or are you going to just bask in all this?" Smith watched the two future starts.

"Pizza!!" Matte headed to the car.

"Okay, let's roll. We'll meet you and Matte at the hut?"

"Okay, John, see you there."

CODE BLUE ICSU ROOM 432, CODE BLUE ICSU ROOM 432....

The dreaded lone voice throughout the hospital.

As Barry grabbed the lifepak and sprinted to the double doors, he called out, "Kurt, watch my two patients. They're both asleep and shouldn't need anything!" That's about all the notice that you get when you cover for the code team.

"Okay, Barry. I'm on it." Kurt waved his hand.

"The coronary care unit's job is to answer all *Code Blues*. This is what we call when a patient is dying or is hemodynamically compromised." Palmer explained to Shelley, a nursing student from the University who is in training on the unit.

"It is our job as the Cardiac Care (CCU) nurse to bring the lifepak and cardiac defibrillator, which are the *paddles* you see and hear about on any medical show. The nurse connects the patient to the monitor, determines the rhythm, and cardio defibrillates the patient if need be."

"Oh, just like on TV - you hear, set for 200 joules, clear, and bang."

"Yes, Shelley. The patient has this jerking motion because the electrical current just went through the body. This is all before the automated defibrillators that you can now see in airports or local malls. What you don't often see on TV is the correct procedure for Advance Cardiac Life Support (ACLS). You'll learn this once you become a registered nurse." Palmer provided the play-by-play of a code to Shelley.

"Usually the patient has an intravenous, breathing tube or ambu bag to provide oxygen. Then, three successive defibrillations of 200, 300, then, if needed, 360 joules, chest compressions, and an epinephrine IV imjection." Katlin joined the conversation.

"The CCU nurse usually runs the code with the doctor, unless we have an ICU nurse who wants to run it. Which is great, we have a great relationship with the ICU and its nursing staff. The Intensive Care Unit (ICU) nurse starts the intravenous lines and assists with the administration of all drugs, fluids, and the like. We also have a respiratory technician (RT) on the team to administer the oxygen requirements."

"So, everyone has a job at each code right?" Shelley took a couple mental notes.

"Yeah, the Emergency Room (ER) doctor and nurse round out the team. Depending on the doctor in the ER, we usually need to offer our suggestions on how to treat the patient. The Critical Care Nurse possesses knowledge of pharmacology, biology, physiology, psychology, you name it. The Certified Critical Care Registered Nurse (CCRN) needs all those skills and the ability to use critical thinking and assessment to work in critical care." Katlin continued the teaching moment.

"The more seasoned nurses are sometimes as knowledgeable as most doctors and certainly all resident and interns. In my twenty-seven years as a nurse, I have only met a handful of interns who possess the skills to function in the critical care units. Those few will ask questions, where the others think they already know everything. Those are the ones who get burnt and risk a fatal outcome. They have done one or two codes, where we do three to four each week." Palmer tag teamed Shelley's learning opportunity.

"Do you only have nurses in CCU or ICU?" Shelley looked at Palmer.

"Administration tries to replace nurses with LPNs or non-nursing personnel. Studies have proven that an RN at the bedside saves lives and shortens hospital stay times, which, in turn, saves money and opens beds for the next patient. That's my rant for now!" Palmer got the last word in.

"We walk the halls and take stairs, so we know each unit and floor and where we need to be in these critical situations." Katlin was still in teaching mode.

"This hospital is a trauma II hospital and one of the largest Cardiac hospitals in the region. So, you will see more registered nurses, BSN, MS and Nurse Practitioners than in many places," Palmer started in on his geography lesson.

"Are you from around here, Shelley?" Palmer questioned Shelley.

"No, I came from Arizona."

"The South Regional trauma hospital is the hospital to work at in southern Colorado. I like the area because we are tucked away in the four corners area, which is a region composed of the northwestern corner of New Mexico, the southeastern corner of Utah, the southwestern corner of Colorado, and the northeastern corner of Arizona. The city itself is a more rural area, but it serves the need to treat the population in this area, which requires a large, major hospital center."

"Wow, you know your area, Palmer."

The Game

"Yes, Professor Palmer, tell us more." Katlin enjoyed Palmer's lessons.

Palmer looked at Katlin and smiled. "The hospital is divided into two sides, for the most part—A wing and B wing, with a few extra beds on the D and E wings. Up on the seventh floor, for some reason, the architects named the floors b and c but is still CSU and SCU. The hospital is large with 550 beds total – Even though there are only six floors above ground and one floor below ground. The basement level has the radiology department, laboratory, emergency room, and a few offices, like administration, College of Physicians, personnel department, and the linen/CSR (Central Supply room). The basement is a great place to go for a walk and clear your head because on nights, it is quiet and no one is around to bother you. The Cardiac Cath lab is one floor up on the main floor"

Palmer continued. "In 1886, the town was built to provide housing for the men working on the tunnels and irrigation ditches that were required to divert water out of the Dolores River and into Montezuma Valley. The town was named for Spanish conquistador Hernán Cortés.

The population is not large, but with the tourists and surrounding area, this makes for the perfect location for such an outstanding medical center. Many doctors want to work here because it is one of the premier heart centers."

"Okay, that's enough, Palmer. I'm sure Shelley will talk to a realtor if she stays." Katlin laughed at Palmer while Shelley smiled.

"Barry, DON'T! Too late." Bev held her ears with both hands.

Crash! Barry gave the doors his usual karate kick to the mid-handles. Bam, the doors flew open, and he's gone like some sort of superhero wannabe who cannot seem to get it right.

"Man, one of these days, we won't have any doors for him to crash through." Bev barked out from inside her patient's room. "One of these days, I am going to smack that kid!"

He's just like that skinny nerd Sheldon from The Big Bang Theory. They can't tell him anything either!"

Barry has been a nurse for only three or four years. He came over from the orthopaedic floor for more excitement. Like all critical care nurses, he went through the critical care course. That's where I first met Barry. I teach the critical care course to the newbies. This is a gruelling six months of classroom and practical work. Once the Nurse completes a few weeks of the class, they buddy with a senior CCU nurse. The buddy does most of the work, mostly to ensure the patient doesn't die from something stupid the newbie would do. We start each class off with a pretest to get a sense of what people know. Barry was the guy who asked questions, worked hard, but still did not seem to have a handle on critical care. No matter what I did to answer his questions, he still missed the point. But he had potential for critical thinking, which is what a good critical care nurse must possess. This nurse has the ability to piece together the big picture. You must ask, what is going on with the organs, and you must be able to understand what the cellular changes are. If you cannot understand the body and how it works, you are just a licensed practitioner (LPN). The fast track to health care. Some kids take a twenty-seven-credit-hour course and think they can operate like a registered nurse, who has more than 120 credit hours. However, I have met some qualified LPNs in my time. A critical care nurse does not stop at the diploma or BSN. This type of nurse reads journals, understands research, and applies this knowledge to each and every patient. I know many nurses who could stand toe-to-toe with many general practitioners, many of them with a lot fewer letters behind their name.

"Don't you train these jackasses to stay calm and relaxed, Palmer?" Bev was still annoyed by Barry's exit. "You should add that to the critical care curriculum."

Barry started in CCU just after I started to teach the critical care course. When I came to the South Regional trauma centre, I was already known for my instructions as a nurse educator and my experience. Barry seemed to have a tough time understanding a few of the principals regarding physiology.

Don't get me wrong. Barry is a great person and will do anything you ask or need. He's great for getting things, setting up rooms, and holding instruments. He likes to feel like he's part of the group, and he will always offer to help. He is a little short with patients and family because he is unsure of what to say or how to explain things to them. He lives by himself, owns a small home up in the west area of town, the West Downey area. He's very proud to be paying off his mortgage and to have money to save…never spends an extra dime. "You just never know what might happen, and you need money" Barry's words, not mine. Barry is very passionate about his collection of guns, and has trouble understanding why not everyone owns at least one gun. He is a member of the NRA, but, for the life of me, I do not know why he is not the president of the NRA.

The first time Barry invited me over to his house, he showed me his roomful of guns and ammo.

"Let's go to the range and we can shoot a few rounds Palmer, it will be fun."

"Yeah let's do it Barry, I don't think I have ever shot a hand gun."

Barry loaded up several of his guns, you name it, and he had it. Hand guns, semis, M-1 Carbine. He had a Dirty Harry gun that was going to be my first gun I try.

"Okay, point it down the course and slowly squeeze the trigger. You should use two hand.

"Okay, Barry. I'll do as you say." Next thing I saw was the post exploding as I hit the two-by-four post that had the target on it.

"Wow, no way! That is so cool! I can see how this may leave a mark." Laughing as I held the gun ready for my next shot.

"I'm coming to your house if we're ever invaded."

Barry just laughed.

Barry used to be a loner outside of the hospital. I think the hospital was his entire world. He loved everything about a hospital. He came to work forty-five minutes early and left thirty minutes after everyone else. He picked up every extra shift available, and he made a ton of money. I always thought of Barry as a good friend, yet it seemed difficult for him to strike up a conversation.

When he met Ingrid Zimmer, he started to see the outside world. Ingrid moved here from Altoona, Pennsylvania. She had worked in ICU for almost five years before moving

The Game

here. Barry liked her from the start. Barry is shy and it took a few months for Barry to actually get the nerve up to ask Ingrid out for a date. He and I talked about Ingrid, and I could tell he was crazy about her, but his social skills needed some help.

She was the one who did it for him. Ingrid is a great person, good nurse, and well-liked by all. Ingrid looks like one of those pretty, plus-size models you see on TV. But, she's super smart. Although you'd never know it until after you get to know her a little bit, or you piss her off and she unleashes her wrath. Many people underestimate these types of people, maybe because of their looks, size, and ethnic background. Ingrid is much more relaxed than Barry, which is why they do well together. Ingrid worked on the day shift, so they would see each other during report.

"Palmer, I'm going to ask Ingrid on a date this week. We have been talking during reports, and I really like her. I think she likes me."

"That's great, buddy, you should. Let me know how it goes."

"Okay, I'm not sure how to start the conversation with her."

"Just talk, man, it will come."

Barry and Ingrid started to date. But yes, it was Ingrid that asked Barry out. It started with just a coffee, but very quickly, they both learned they had much in common. They both liked camping, BBQ, and guns. They go out on dates to the shooting range for target practice. They make a great pair.

Barry started to kick the front doors of the unit after he was called on a code blue one night and could not open the door because he was carrying the lifepak in one hand and using the other to wedge the pager in his pocket. BANG! He hit the door and fell over. We all laughed so hard, I thought we might need to be revived ourselves. The problem with Barry being so hyped up on the calls that he runs is that everything is swinging and out of control. He usually loses all the gel pads that are needed to defibrillate the patient before he arrives at the bedside. We have asked Barry many times to slow down, think, and react. Barry interprets this as, react! Or, as the saying goes, "shoot first and ask questions later."

"Barry, just slow down. Think about what's needed, then react. Use your critical thinking skills." I would tell Barry more often than not.

One night when Barry went busting out the door and dropped a couple gel pads on the way out, the rest of decided to have some fun at his expense.

"Let's have some fun." Franco grabbed extra gel pads from the counter in the corner where the lifepak is kept.

"Yeah, let's lay the pads all the way to the stairs." Bev laughed as she joined Franco.

Franco laid out several pads all the way to the stairs. When all was done, it looked like a Hansel and Gretel trail of breadcrumbs so Barry could find his way back to the unit.

"Let's just go about our work when he comes in." Katlin announced to all.

"Well, I guess I'll see if his patients are alive." Kurt laughed with his best mountain-man voice and lumbered over to room 4, where Mr. Novato had been resting after his angioplasty.

The Game

Barry came back the same way he left and saw all the pads on the floor. His face got redder and redder with every pad he picked up.

"What the hell?" Barry held all the pads in his hands and dropped them as he walked in the door.

"Who did this? You guys are a bunch of assholes." Barry replaced the lifepak and threw the pads on the counter.

We all burst into laughter. "Barry, what's wrong?" Franco was still laughing.

"Hey, rookie! Welcome to the team," Bev smiled and gave Barry a big hug.

"You guys are still assholes," Barry now laughed as well.

"Okay, kid. We couldn't resist." Katlin moved to her room to check on her patient.

"Barry, your patients are all okay still." Kurt smiled at Barry.

Barry's patient, Mr. Novato, has been lying flat for almost four hours and will soon be able to move after bed rest is over. This is the standing order from *the Group*. Mr. Novato had his angioplasty performed by the Heart group.

The Heart group is a group of about twenty cardiologists who leave the femoral arterial line in for us to monitor the blood pressure and draw blood work, as needed. We all know the docs leave the line in case the coronary artery and or stent closes and they can quickly gain access. This group of cardiologists includes some of the best in the nation. Problem is, they know it and let everyone else know it as well. They will try things that make the other cardiology groups quiver. Nevertheless, they save lives, and, if I have a heart attack, I would want them standing over me.

"Mr. Novato, please, lay down. ... NO, DO NOT pull on that!"

One thing you learn while working in CCU, is when someone says don't pull on that, usually it is one of two things; the catheter to pee through or the arterial line.

DON'T pull on that!" Kurt shouted, which drew us all, and we started to walk to the patient's room.

Sometimes the patient will get at the Endotracheal Tube (ET) and pull on that. That's always fun, because now you have to not only sedate the patient, but attempt to re intubate before anything really bad happens.

"Hey, what's up, Kurt? Need some help?" Bev was the first to get there.

"No, I think I'm good."

"Okay, holler if you want me." Bev gave a shout as she headed back to a chair to work on her report and assessment.

"Hey, gimmy a hand over here!" Franco demanded, as he always does.

"Sure, what's up?" Palmer headed to Franco's room.

"Ah, I need to turn this turd." As they walked toward the room, and definitely not in ear shot of the patient.

Mr. Maestes is no little turd. Mr. Maestes is about 300 pounds and just had bypass surgery. It takes both of us with a little help from Bev—she hadn't gotten to her reports, but had gotten up from the chair to assist.

After surgery patients tend to need help turning so we prop pillows around the patient to keep them as comfortable as possible. Maestes was overflow from the SICU that night.

"Okay, you guys pull, and I'll tuck the pillows" Franco fluffed his pillow.

The Game

That's the perk you get when it's your room and your patient. So, Franco stuffed pillows behind the patient's back and between his legs, and he readjusted the head pillow, so Mr. Maestes could drool a little easier.

"Hey, thanks guys, that went easy," Franco smiled because he didn't have to pull on the patient.

"Yeah, sure, no problem," Bev remarked sarcastically, holding her lower back.

"I hate all this heavy work we do," Bev commented on the duty to ensure the patients don't fall or injure themselves. "The number one problem with most nurses is our backs. Patients believe they can put their full weight on us, like we're leaning posts. They expect us to pick them up, carry them around. Administration cannot understand why there are so many injuries on the job. I would like to see them come down off their ivory tower and try this," Bev still steamed.

"But that's administration. Always looking to save a buck. They were looking at the big picture. Funding for the hospital. If accreditation is not met, the hospital would lose millions of dollars. So, we always had a bean counter coming around to make sure no one was creating waves that would jeopardize the accreditation. They even watched us. If we were sick or an incident occurred, they would try to cover it up. If we had a pre-existing disease or problem, they would not cover us. It appeared as if they did not want to pay out any expenses or benefits to us." Palmer played devil's advocate.

"If the hospital lost its accreditation, the hospital would lose funding, which was in the millions. So it was in the best interest of the hospital to make it look like all was well.

Administrators showed us slides and gave handouts on what to say and how to act when the accreditors came through. It was always tense. One too many deaths or lawsuits would give a failing grade." Palmer finished his thought.

"You must be lifting wrong. Let us teach you how.... Haven't we all heard that before?" Franco added to the conversation.

"Piss off. The fact of the matter is that nurses are abused by patients, family, administration, and doctors." Bev gave Franco her best glare.

"Yeah, tell that to my back." I think we need a chiropractor on duty," Bev moaned and groaned her way out the door.

Kurt came out of Barry's patient's room and was ready to do his reports. Things had calmed down a little.

I think we do have a great group of nurses in our permanent weekend night shift. We all pitch in to help. Most units start people on nights and slowly move them to days. In this hospital, you worked days or you worked nights. Very few staff members would do both. So many of us liked one shift or the other. For the six of us, we loved weekend nights. Thursday to Sunday night, every week. We all became great friends and did many things together. We became the best nurses and team in the hospital. The emergency docs would call up to see if we were on and would be responding to the code blue. Cardiology doctors knew if we were on, they would sleep easy knowing their patients were in our hands. We had it made in CCU/SICU. We got everything—new equipment, drug rep meals, gifts, all sorts of stuff. We had the run of the hospital. If we said we were full, no one tried to push a patient on us. Our docs never allowed anyone but cardiology to admit to the seventh floor. Those were the cardiologist's and thoracic surgery beds, end of story. The main floor has the Cath lab, echo department, ECG, and pacer department. The seventh floor is all cardiac—the coronary care unit, and the surgical ICU, which is mostly coronary artery bypass and thoracic-type stuff. The surgical patients recover in SICU, then go to SSU.

"One day Administration will spend millions on reworking the whole flow of the hospital. They're even thinking of moving the units, so the operating rooms and the Cardiac Cath lab would all be located on one floor. Should be fun." Katlin chimed in on the situation. "The bottom line is cardiology makes big money. That is what Administration pushed in advertising our facility. People would donate huge sums of money to the hospital; people trusted this hospital with their health and the administration with their money. Government does fund the hospital as long as the accreditation is current, and the administrators accepted non-insured patients. The hospital made sure we all understood the consequences of maintaining the accreditation and the good name of the hospital." Katlin towed the administrative line.

"So how did it go this time, kid?" our fearless leader, Katlin, asked Barry, as if she didn't know.

"Uh, well... he died." Barry stated mournfully, as if he had just lost another close friend.

"Well, what can you do, kid"? Katlin replied. She well knew that there is never much that we can do. If we did bring patients back from the dead, there is only about 10 percent chance they would walk out of the hospital. Nevertheless, it is sure nice to see when they do. "I'm sure you did everything you could."

"How did the code go?" again, Katlin knew the answer full well

"Well, I had trouble with the defibrillator again…I pushed the deactivation button instead of the discharge button. I think he may have a few fractured ribs as well.… I …ahh… I may have pushed too hard on compressions. I always take too long to calculate the doses for dopamine and Isuprel infusions, so we never did get the drugs into him. The ICU nurse had to help with that."

Perhaps one of these days, we might tell Barry that in a code, calculations are not a high priority. We always start the drug and titrate until we get a response. Once you save the guy, then you can back off and calculate titrations in CCU. But, that's me, I had a doctor tell me that once.

"Oh well," Katlin calmed Barry down, "I'm sure he was old and not long for this world."

"Hey, Kurt, how's my patient doing?" Barry asked as he slipped back into the early morning CCU routine, and not wanting to rehash the code.

"He's okay, but watch him—he was tugging on his arterial line. Last thing you want is the femoral artery bleeding if this gets pulled out."

"Okay. Thanks for watching, Kurt."

Katlin starts all shifts by coming in early. She enjoys the evening calm. Once inside the building, she climbs the seven flights of stairs that she often thinks were once easier to climb. Katlin enjoys a coffee as she calmly sits at the huge round table, listening to the bells and alarms on the unit, and letting the steam fog her glasses.

"Hey, Katlin. In early again to check up on us?" Melissa noted that Katlin already had a chart open.

"No, just a habit of mine. I like looking through charts."

When the doctors see that Katlin is on, they know it will be a quiet night. She taught me to think beyond the patient, looking at what happens at a cellular level. "For every action, you get a reaction," she always said. If you show interest, then she will too. Nothing is worse than being charge of a group of blond wannabes who never seem to understand what it is to be a registered nurse. Many of the doctors ask her age, but she always replies "way too young for you." If I was dying, I would want her working on me. Not only because she is a great nurse, but also it would be nice to open your eyes and see her over top of you. Katlin actually took time off and came back to nursing. Katlin basically put her husband through collage as a physician assistant. She took care of the house, the husband, and her child while working for the insurance company. Katlin, workaholic, smart, could have been a doctor, but she chose to be a nurse. Stayed home to raise her daughter. Married to Jason who is never home.

Therefore, it is usually just Katlin and her now seventeen-year-old daughter who hold down the five-acre homestead. They ride horses, so it is nice to have a little room. Meghan is Katlin's daughter. She is a great rider and rides in various horse shows around the state. Katlin's husband was never around for many of the usual events that a father should be at. Katlin knew many people and many were guys who wanted to know her better. She did show interest in a few guys but never talked much about herself and the problems at home.

Katlin is one of the mentors in CCU. She will quiz you about anything and everything. For a while, when I ran on codes, she made me feel it was me who did something wrong. The more I worked with her, the more I came to understand the reality, and her sense of humor. People die. Only about 10 percent of the people who code in the hospital make it out and go home. I eventually learned that Katlin would tease the ones she liked and knew you would grow from her comments. I saw this way back when she came back to the hospital, it's one of her many qualities.

"Okay, guys and gals, if you are all done playing with your patients, please give me an update"

Did I mention Katlin is always done first, making a great team leader? Her room is always the cleanest and neatest… always! Her patients come first and foremost. She works hard on each patient like each one is a relative. As a team lead, she knows everything about each patient. She visits each patient and talks to the relatives of all our patients. Katlin is loved by all. Perhaps that is what draws me to her.

"My guy sucks… I always get the fat ones," Franco complained. Franco complains even when he gets the young skinny patients. "My patient is doing well. I think in the next couple of days he'll be ready to transfer out."

"Thanks, Franco. I'll pass that on to the day shift in the morning." Katlin was writing notes on the report page.

Franco came to the Southwest region Hospital from Boston. Franco was born and raised in Boston. I asked Franco once why he came out west.

The Game

"To damn cold in Mass. I wanted to come someplace warm, so we came here."

He met his wife in Boston, and they moved to the four corners area for the fun of it. Franco is the crazy one on the team. He would kick anyone's ass, but you say the word and he is there for you. Franco is a smart nurse and works hard from start to finish. He has a few creative pharmacology cocktails he provides to his patients. It's a mystery if he did this so he did not get bothered all night, or if the patients truly needed them. Either way, his patients were quiet. One thing he loves to use is Milk of Magnesia on this patient's butt. Said it healed any irritation down there.

Franco talks about sex all the time. He discusses any and all details at any given time. The first time he talked about what he did to his wife…. "Oh, man, I had fun last night" Franco grinned from ear to ear. There was no point in ignoring him because he would follow you around just to get his story in.

"I waited till Ang fell asleep and pulled all the covers off … THEN…."

"Franco, wait till the respiratory therapist leaves," I said with a little embarrassment.

"Hey, it's okay if she hears," Franco stated, still grinning ear to ear.

Funny thing was, so was the RT. "Hey it's not like I haven't seen or heard this before," the respiratory technician laughed.

"Anyway, then I slowly opened her legs and slid my hand down between her legs. Once I opened her up, I got on top and went to town!"

"Did she wake up?" I asked innocently.

"Why yes, I know I was awake at that point!" Ang commented.

"Yeah, then I came! WOW, that was fun. The next thing I know she throws me over and said..."

"How dare you start without me!" blurted out the RT, as if she had been there or something.

I looked over at the RT, and she was smiling as if she obviously knew something I did not.

"Oh, you already sat through his story, yeah." I knew I was not the first person that Franco had cornered.

"No, but once I threw Franco off me, I jumped him, and we didn't sleep all day...and now, here we are."

"Palmer, close your mouth. You look a little surprised" Franco laughed.

"Well, I am. I thought you said you were married?"

"I am, Palmer. Meet Ang, my wife."

That was back when I first met the pair. The two were fun to be around, and although their stories sometimes seemed to go a little overboard, they meant no harm. Together or separately, they would always help you out, and, in no time, they became part of our circle of comrades.

Outside of work, we all had our own thing. But, on occasion, we met up for golf, parties, and on this day, we moved me into my new house.

"Guys, I have an amazing opportunity for you this week. I found a new house on the west side of town. Who wants to join me for a house-warming party?"

"What's the opportunity, Palmer?" Kurt and Franco asked at the same time.

The Game

"I need help moving my stuff and you guys are the best at it, so I hear."

"Okay, I'll help you move if there's beer and food," Kurt demanded.

"Sure, I'll have it all ready for after we finish moving all the stuff."

"Okay, count me in too," said Franco as he walked away from the conversation.

"Hey, can I hang out with you guys?" Barry joined in.

"Sure, no problem, Barry."

"I also asked Thomas to join us."

"Why are you moving Palmer?" Barry asked out of shear curiosity.

"This house came on the market. It's quiet, new, and away from the city."

Asking buddies to move is sometimes a good thing and sometimes shit happens. Loading the truck seemed easy. Piling boxes on top of each other is the easy part. Loading furniture is tricky. So that week, we met at my apartment and made a plan for loading the truck.

"Let's start with the big stuff guys, then we can stuff the smaller things between the couch and in corners." I had to direct these guys.

"Barry, come help me move the bed. It should go in first." Franco took over the operation.

"Hey, Palmer, this bed doesn't look like it's seen much action." Franco laughed.

"Oh, man, that's heavy, Franco." Barry did some stretches and warmed up like a weight lifter, not understanding Franco's snide comment.

"Okay, what's next?" Kurt asked.

"Well, let's get the couch, chairs, and then the tables." Palmer pointed at the living room.

"Check, let's get at it", Kurt headed to the couch.

In no time at all, we had packed the truck up with most items. The move or rather loading the truck had been simple, and we all stood admiring our work. Then *BANG*. The furniture shifted, and the coffee table collapsed.

"Well, you have to expect settling on loads like this."

"Thanks, Kurt. That's good to know." My tone was a little sarcastic, but my dad had made the table when I first moved out on my own – and it had become an old friend, having seen me through many girlfriends, dogs, dates, and pizza nights.

We arrived at the new house and unloading was quick. I think mostly so we could get to the keg of beer I had on ice. The most important piece in the move was the stereo. No one touched it or came close to it. Palmer carried in each piece and set it up as soon as possible.

"No one touches the stereo. This is my baby. I love music. It relaxes me."

"Wow, you have a wide variety of vinyl." Barry thumbed through the LPs.

"Stop right there, do not touch my LPs, Barry." Palmer half smiled.

"You have Wynton Marsalis. He plays jazz, right?"

"Yes, Barry. I love jazz, please put it down."

"Wow, Fleetwood Mac, Billy Holiday, Diana Kroll."

"Yes Barry. I have a very broad variety of music and artists."

"Palmer is this a NAD C558?" Thomas was looking at the turntable.

"Yeah, I have a NAD C558. It has a reputation for precision engineering that makes music sound amazing—it's even built on a solid MDF base with rubber feet to minimize vibration."

"The nine-inch aluminum tone arm with a premounted Ortofon OM10 cartridge! This turntable is a beauty, Palmer. It comes complete with this gold-plated RCA audio jack with detachable phono cable, high-gloss black lacquer finish, and fully manual operation."

"Wow, Thomas. You know your equipment. Thanks for the sales pitch" I said standing next to Thomas and smiled at his stereo manual's description.

"Enough of this BS, let's crack that keg out." Franco headed to the keg with a glass.

"Okay, guys. Thanks for helping, let's have a drink or two."

We opened the keg and had several drinks. Looking out the front window, you could see the bluff just down a block or so.

"Let's go sit up on the bluff; we can sit up there and look down on everyone." Franco refilled his drink before the climb.

"Sure, it's easy to walk up to the top. I've been up there a few times already." I laughed as I headed over for a refill.

We all filled our drinks and walked up the side of the bluff.

"Wow! Look at all these sharp rocks, looks like an explosion happened and left this pile of boulders and rocks all over." Kurt admired throughout the hike up the bluff.

The sun was setting over the houses, casting long shadows and shapes. Sitting at the top, everything looked so orange and red from the setting sun.

"Do you know any neighbors yet?" Thomas looked at the few houses at the bottom.

"No, but another guy from the hospital might be moving in over at the end of the road. I think it will be quiet here."

"Yeah, this will be great for bringing home chicks, right?" Franco sipped on his remaining half glass.

"Who's that girl you been seeing from the hospital? What is her name; she works on the fourth floor, doesn't she?" Franco continued.

"Ah, no one. I don't have a girlfriend."

"Good, you can bring a new one home each night." Kurt laughed at Franco's comments.

"I need another beer. Barry, want to come with me?

"No Franco. I'm good."

"Anyone? Well the hell with you, I'm going for one." Franco started straight down the bluff.

"I'm okay, no worries." Franco laughed as he headed back for another drink.

"Franco, go slow or you will fall." Thomas watched as Franco stumbled.

The next step was the funniest. Franco tripped and went down the bluff head over heels. We may have had one too many drinks because we all laughed and watched Franco fall, stand up, and then fall again.

"I'm okay." Franco laughed after each somersault.

"We better go down and make sure he's still alive." Thomas stood up and looked down the bluff.

The Game

The guys had a couple more drinks and left. Franco was in the house asleep on the couch.

"Hey, buddy, ready to go home? It's getting late" Palmer shook Franco.

"The guys have left already."

"Sure, but can you drive me home? Ang will drive you back." Franco slurred his words.

"Sure, let's roll." Jumping into Franco's car.

The ride was quiet because Franco was sleeping. I arrived at Franco's house and he woke up as the car stopped. He got out of the car. "Thanks, man, see you tomorrow."

Ang gave me a ride home, which was quiet as well. I think she might have been mad at our drinking.

The next day at work, Ang gave me shit, screaming "what the hell did you do to Franco?"

"Nothing, why"?

"He came home with his back all cut up from falling down that stupid hill. Only I get to scratch his back!" Ang laughed while trying to be serious.

They had no children, and they liked it that way. They could come and go as they please.

"Franco, what's up with your kids?" Katlin reminded us that we were professionals and that we should be focused on our work…

"I turned him at two, and he was sleeping… vital signs are stable, chest tubes come out tomorrow, and he should go to SSU in the morning." Franco's patient was an overflow from SICU. We take bypass patients every once in a while. We also take every heart and heart/lung transplant in CCU. The surgeons want a clean, sterile environment for these patients, and CCU fit the bill. We need to be ready for anything. We are a coronary care unit first, but we have had head trauma patients who had large surgeries that require extra anesthetic or medication to maintain blood pressure,

"Great! We need the room as there are a few Caths on the list," Katlin announced, without looking up from her report sheet.

We can always count on a few patients coming from the Cath lab with an arterial line. There is always the concern about the stents collapsing. The first twenty-four hours after a stent placement are critical. If a stent is going to close, it's during this time period. We always try to keep an open bed for the Percutaneous Coronary Intervention (PCI) procedures that became complicated and go to the OR. Same with an ER patient that comes in with a heart attack, we try to be ready for anything, but mostly we have to play it by ear.

"Hi! This is Sandra from the ER. We will be getting a husband and wife from a Motor Vehicle Incident (MVI) outside of town. The wife was driving, suffered a heart attack, and crashed."

The ER doc still had to call the cardiac doc to get the okay to bring these two up to us. The husband had a head trauma; he was critical, but stable. The wife was touch-and-go. They weren't sure if she would make the night. We had to scramble to transfer one patient out to the floor to make room for both. That required doubling up on the patient per nurse ratio. We never like to take a fresh patient with another patient. You just never know how much time a new

The Game

admit will take. We can't ignore a patient in CCU, therefore switching staff and patient assignments was a routine for us.

We received the husband first; he had a head injury and was on his way to the OR for burr holes. (They drill holes in the head to relieve pressure) We had to go to the ER to assist with lines and tubes for the wife. We got the wife up, and she coded on us. We spent hours working on her. We had all the usual drugs hanging, Dopamine, Isuprel, blood, saline, you name it. Nothing seemed to stabilize her. Dr. Hunter finally called the code because there was no heartbeat. Dr. Hunter went to the family to let them know their mom had died. This is never a good time. Family always believe that once the family members make it to a hospital, the patient will live and walk out of here. Meantime, Stacey and I were just ready to shut everything off, when the patient took a breath and a heartbeat showed up on the monitor. Stacey and I both raced to check the breathing and pulse.

"Damn, she's still alive! Stacey, go quick and head off Dr. Hunter before she tells the family that their mom's dead"

Stacey ran through the doors like a track star. Meantime, Victor the respiratory technician and I hooked her back to the vent and got the lines running again. We calculated the drips per minute for the dopamine and decreased the Isuprel. Both Stacey and Dr. Hunter came running back in.

"What the hell is going on?" I was about to tell the family that their mother had died."

"Out of the blue, she had a pulse and took a few breaths, so we put her back on the respirator" I said in amazement.

"Okay, let's get her stable. Then I can go and tell the family a little good news," Dr. Hunter said as she checked the vital signs. Dr. Hunter is a good doctor, she works hard, and we all like her, but she is still a little unsure of herself. That's why she calls us to assist in the ER when she is not sure. We can and always do suggest what should be done. Most doctors like when we can suggest different strategies. Most doctors have come to learn and trust what we say. Our weekend night shift takes pride in the knowledge we have and the time we spend developing our skills and knowledge of the human body, physiology, and pharmacology.

We got Mrs. Carlyle stable in time to greet Mr. Carlyle back from the OR. Mr. Carlyle progressed very well over the weeks. He was finally discharged to the step-down unit. However, his wife struggled for weeks, on and off the ventilator. The sad conclusion was she recovered and was transferred to the step-down unit, where she died shortly thereafter.

"Kurt, what's up with your two?" Katlin worked her way around the table.

"Sleeping, I have no immediate concerns," Kurt gave his usual statement.

Kurt gets away with these abbreviated reports, only because he is 90 percent correct. I know only two people who are smarter than Kurt.

"Okay, let me know when things become more immediate" Katlin replied, knowing exactly what he meant.

"Hey, Barry, care to join our little soiree?" Katlin smiled as she asked him. The unit may have private rooms, but they have very thin walls, making it easy to talk to anyone in the room, or if need be to call out to the main desk area.

The Game

"Uhh... well... uh. ... Oh, crap! No, I need some. ...Don't pull on that Mr... SHIT!"

"Clean up in aisle five, clean up in aisle five," Kurt laughed as we all ran to room 5 in time to see the blood hit the ceiling.

Mr. Novato had pulled his arterial line out. You can always tell how high a blood pressure is by the spray of the blood on the wall. Mr. Novato's blood hit the wall only once before we made it to the end of the bed. Fortunately, we got a hand on the artery before the patient passed out.

Just another night in Seventh Heaven.

CODE BLUE CSU, CODE BLUE CSU…

Because the code is on the seventh floor, often a couple of us will run to help out.

The code blue team, all except for the doctor, answer the call to CSU. Dr. DePaul, the emergency doctor on duty this night was not the best of doctors on staff. He did not believe it was his job to run after patients in the hospital, so he would finish whatever he was doing in the ER prior to coming to the code.

Patty came up from ER and stated "Dr. DePaul will be along shortly. He had to remove an ingrown toenail from a patient, or something stupid like that."

Unwilling to wait for Dr. DePaul, Betty from ICU and I ran the code. We followed the Advance Cardiac Life Support guidelines (ACLS), as we usually do. Connect the patient to the monitor, and while I was doing that the ICU nurse started the lines, RT starts *bagging the patient* to provide oxygen to the patient. We shocked the patient three times, then started the IV meds. We shock the patient again and continue with chest compressions. Victor from Respiratory intubated the patient and taped the tube down. Again, this allows for 100 percent oxygen to the patient.

"This fifty-six-year old male was admitted for angina." The floor Nurse shouted out to all in the room.

The patient was in a rhythm called Ventricular Tachycardia at a rate of about 250 BPM.

"We have to run magnesium and potassium to help stabilize the heart rhythm, right guys? Betty asked the team to concur. We stabilized the patient, made room in the CCU for the patient, and called the cardiologist on call to come assess the patient. Things were going fine until Dr. DePaul stormed the door and screamed at us,

"How dare you push medications and intubate a patient without a doctor present!" Dr. DePaul was really using a new vocabulary at us. This went on and on until Dr. Frank Bennett came out of the newly arrived patient's room.

"What the HELL is all the barking out here?" Dr. Frank Bennett is a young, hard-working, amazing cardiologist. He completed his residency up in Calgary, Alberta. He is originally from Kentucky, cowboy boots, and that southern accent. Great family man. If I have a heart attack, I want him at the Cath lab table. I once saw him stent a left main coronary artery, which at the time was new and extremely risky.

Before Dr. DePaul could say a word, Dr. Bennett walked over to Dr. DePaul and laid into him.

"You son of a bitch, these guys saved your and the patient's behind, and you're too stupid to realize this?" You take your sorry ass back down to the ER and finish your ingrown toenails because this will be the last shift you do"

The Game

Needless to say, Dr. DePaul was never seen of or heard from again. Dr. Bennett is a great cardiologist and well respected in town. He works hard, expects nothing short of perfection, and lets you know if you did well… or not.

It was common for us to push ACLS medications. That's what we are trained to do. With that much Experience in one room, it's hard to argue. The patient lived and walked out of the hospital.

CHAPTER TWO

HOW WE PLAY THE GAME

"Hi, Mary. Where's Bob?" Katlin asked as she entered Mary's room.

"Oh my, Katlin, thanks for stopping in. Bob's down getting coffee. How are you?"

"Good. Sorry I couldn't make it back last night, we got a little busy."

"The doctor said all went well, and I will probably go home soon."

"Yeah, I looked at your chart before coming in."

"Yes, of course, you did. Did you uncover any mysteries?" Mary laughed.

"No, your labs are near normal. I see they started you on a medication that is used for stents. It's called Clopidogrel. It's a platelet aggregation inhibitor. It gives the body time to cover the stent, or medically speaking, endothelialisation of the stent. You will be off that medication after a while."

"Yeah, the doctor said I would be taking something for the stent."

"You get some rest. I'll talk to you soon. Say hi to Bob, luv you both."

"Thanks, Kate. Luv you too. Thank you for being there."

"No problem, dear. You've been there many times for me."

"Yes, speaking of which, how's your situation?"

"Oh well, you know. Doing things on my own. It may be permanent if I ever decide to do something."

"You've always been independent and known exactly what you want. Why do you lack confidence in making this decision?"

"Hi, Bob. I was just leaving and thought I might miss you. Take care of this one. Bye." Katlin avoided the question.

"Will do, she's a keeper."

"Hey, you owe me an answer, Miss Kate," Mary shook her finger and laughed.

"One day, one day," Katlin mused as she walked out the door.

"Excuse me, miss. I am looking for the administration office, for a Mr. Glover?"

"Sure, who are you?" Katlin nearly ran into Mr. Smith.

"Mr. Smith, well Detective Smith. I am here to talk to a Mr. Glover."

"Sounds serious, is this about the deaths?" Katlin looked over the unassuming man in front of her.

"Sorry, I did not catch your name, miss."

"Katlin, I work in CCU and just came to talk to my friend."

"Oh" Smith reached into his pocket. "I wanted to talk to you, do you have time? Your name came up in some of the conversations that I've had."

The Game

"Let me take you to Mr. Glover's office. He is actually down a few flights. You are a little way away. We can chat on the way."

"Yeah, I followed the sign in the lobby and ended up here."

"What questions do you have for me? Let's take this elevator, detective." Katlin motioned to the bank of elevators.

"Thanks. Well, what can you tell me about these deaths?" Smith followed Katlin.

"Not much, they all seem very suspicious. I have heard it may be a doctor or nurse."

"Yeah, some say it might even be someone in CCU." Smith flipped through his notes while they waited for the elevator.

"Us! I don't think so. Our team is one of the best in the hospital. We all work together and socialize together."

"Well, yes, you are all very tight. Easy to keep secrets, don't you think?" Smith held the elevator door for Katlin.

"No. It is none of us. I think it is someone that is seen, but dismissed as a familiar person on the floors." Katlin looked at the numbers as the elevator descended.

"Yes, perhaps you're right. Can we talk again? Soon Katlin?"

"Yes, detective. You know where I am, CCU."

"Thanks. Do I go left?"

"Yes, left and look for *Glover* on the door."

I have always needed to arrive early to work, parties, dates, you name it. I arrive about 7:15 p.m., which gives me about fifteen minutes to have a coffee and get into the swing of things. Sometimes that gets me into trouble. One night, I actually arrived at 7:00 p.m., only to see my room full of OR nurses, the physician, and everyone else, running around like lunatics. I poured myself a cup of coffee and watched the ever-entertaining Dr. Walters.

Dr. Walters looks like a middle linebacker for the Dallas Cowboys. He is big, loud, and demanding. Dr. Walters was elbow deep in my patient's chest, trying to tie off a bleeding graft. Victor Torres, the RT, had come in early and was watching the ventilator. Dr. Winnick was giving a couple paralytics to the patient while Karen was feeding Midazolam through the IV tube. Barking orders, Dr. Walters had all the nurses running in and out of the room.

Deb came running by and said "get in there, this is your patient tonight"

The charge nurse knew I always took the sickest patients. The more lines, tubes, and machines, the better. A typical patient who came in, recovered, and went home was of no interest to me. I need the challenge, the adrenaline.

One thing I have learned is do not enter a room without report and confirmation that this is your patient. You don't want to get involved and have your actual patients ignored.

"No way, not until 7:30 p.m. That's when I step in." I sipped my coffee.

"Okay, that will hold until we get back to the operating room," Dr. Walters declared, as people started to pack up the patient and the equipment.

Dr. Walters stepped out of the room and headed toward the coffee. Nolan and I were friends, we played hockey, and talked about sports, so we knew each other. If Dr. Walters did not know you, you had a hard time getting anything out of him but a bad attitude. The Operating Room (OR) team

The Game

was running out the door with my patient, others gathered to have a quick sip of coffee; I thought I would chat…

"Hey, Dr. Walters. Couldn't find any time in the OR, so you have to do surgery out here in my room?" I asked.

Well, a gasp came from the nurses who had just been in the room and had been running like gophers for the last hour.

"What did you say?" Walters demanded in his outside voice.

So, I asked again, "What brings you out here?"

Dr. Walters laughed and said, "Yeah, you're right. We had no room in the OR for this guy, and I didn't really want to go home. Actually, he popped a graft. I kind of thought that would happen. Not very good tissue at the joints. His blood pressure crept up a little too high and bang. When he gets out, I need his blood pressure at about one hundred systolic and no more. We'll worry about his kidneys after he survives the night. You got him"?

"Yeah, I think so."

"You want me to put in a good word for you?" Dr. Walters's smiled away." That way, we make sure you have him for the night."

"No, last time you did that, I ended up staying for eighteen hours, looking after the last one. Thanks, but no thanks."

We all laughed and went in for report, so I could take the patient back when he came out of the OR.

SEVEN THIRTY, EVENING SHIFT CHANGE

Martha is a forty-five-year-old divorced nurse who works night shift at the hospital. The graying of her reddish hair and ashen completion could be due to the numerous cigarettes and occasional drinks of whiskey or even the toll her marriage had on her. Martha knows everything that goes on in the hospital, and outside. At least that is what she tells everyone. These deaths in the hospital have her mind working overtime.

"I know who is killing all our patients." Martha leaned over the break-room table as she blurted out to whomever was listening. "Yep, it's not who the police or the hospital think it is. They want us to believe it's one of us, but it's not"! Martha's rant drew the usual eye rolling and smirks from her coworkers. Martha loved to visit the units to check up on what had been going on as of late. She will come in, chat, and then head back to her floor to start her night.

"Okay, Martha, who is killing our patients?" Janet piped in. "Why would anyone be killing patients?"

"Oh, you would be surprised, Janet. Either we need to open beds to refill them and increase revenue or someone knows these patients and is knocking them off."

"Oh, my god! You think the hospital is hiring someone to knock off patients to make more money?" Janet squealed and shook her head, setting her blond pigtails swaying to the disbelief in her voice.

"You will see." Martha continued, fully confident that she knows who the killer is. "I have already notified the authorities."

The Game

"No, Martha! Not again." Janet sounded like a person who was scolding a pet for peeing on the rug. "But, Martha, this hospital relies on donations and government handouts. If the word gets out that people are being killed in the hospital, all funding and donations will disappear".

Martha now sat up with her hands on her knees and leaned forward. "That's why this is such a secret. Nurses and doctors are all in on it. No one is saying anything."

"I also hear the police are already talking to Katlin."

"Oh, Martha, stop already."

Martha is an old-school nurse. She seems to know everyone and everything about the other nurses and doctors. She's just one of a group of nurses who remind you of neighbourhood busybodies. Mostly, they gossip and speculate about their colleagues to pass the time and one-up each other during their gossip sessions. But Martha is the leader of this gang, and her troops report to her. Living alone with her two cats in a small apartment block just east of the hospital doesn't give her a lot to do, and the layout of the apartment lets her step out the back and see what her neighbours are up to. Gossiping just seems to flourish in that kind of atmosphere.

Katlin entered the report room, or lunch room, whichever you want to call it, depending on what it is needed for at the time.

"Well, Martha, what brings you to our neck of the woods?"

"Nothing, Katlin, just leaving." Martha now stood and gave Katlin a sinister grin.

"Katlin, let me start report." Janet is now disinterested in the gossip and turns her head to Katlin.

Janet is a good-looking—twenty something, blonde hair, and blues eyes. She has worked in critical care for more years than her age, schooling, and work experience would suggest. Janet is very practical, quiet, and professional. At least until she is off work. Who knew that she loved to go out and party?

To be young and single.

"Katlin, here is the list I came up with for your staff tonight. Let me know if you agree once report is done."

"Sure, Janet. As long as I get what I want, I'm happy".

"Katlin, you're funny. I know for a fact you would take what's left. You want your staff to be happy."

"Don't let my secret get out!" laughed Katlin sheepishly.

"How is your friend, Katlin?" Janet asked quietly.

"Oh yeah. She will most likely go home tomorrow. She feels 100 percent better."

"Hey, assholes! Everyone get enough sleep today?" Franco belched out, walking into the report room.

That's Franco's way of saying 'Hi, have a good day today.'

"Hey, Franco. How 'bout you, you sleep?" Barry asked with real concern.

"Well, I didn't sleep a wink," Bev stated as she walked into the report room just behind Franco.

"My boyfriend came over…and over." Bev was still reliving her day with the boyfriend. We never met this guy, but every night we hear about him. Bev lets everyone know this at every opportunity, knowing no one will take her up on this. I've never been sure if he was real or not. Bev is a great gal, but she has one thing on her mind….SEX. They say guys think of sex every eight seconds, well Bev thinks about

The Game

sex every six seconds. The thing is, Bev is a tall strawberry blonde, about twenty-six or so, and someone who loves life and tries to enjoy it at every opportunity.

"Tell me all about it, Bev," Franco asked as he pulled a chair up next to Bev. Franco and Bev were two of a kind. I think if Franco was single, these two would be an item.

"I also went out with Tara the other night over to Logan's. I love eating those peanuts and just tossing them anywhere." Bev added her comment. "I think Tara likes them as well. She filled her pockets with them."

"Are you gals close or something?" Franco still sat close to Bev.

"Yeah, we've been close for many years. We started here about the same time, so we were in orientation together. The rest is history."

"Okay, I see how it is, you're real close!" Franco smiled as he put his lunch in the fridge.

"Oh, Franco, you wish. Get your mind out of the gutter."

"Okay, let's get to it. We have a couple of patients coming, and one just went to the OR," Janet, the day shift charge person announced as she opened her notes.

"Ahhh! Damn. Bev was just going to tell us about her day." Franco explained with a huge grin.

That's the way we did report, the day charge would give an overview of all the patients, then we would go out to the day nurse and get a more detailed report. This routine often took about thirty minutes. Karen, our manager, said the charge person knew best as to which patient was suited to the oncoming nurse. So, it was always worthwhile to be nice to the day charge person.

Don McLean

We have a fairly simple routine in CCU. We come in, get an overview and our assignment for the night, then go out to the floor for the one-to-one report. That's where you get a real feel for your patient or patients.

I only have a few things I need from the day nurse, but I let them speak. It helps us to slowly get into the swing of things at the start of the shift and unwind a little before going home.

Once report is done, I go straight to the chart to read all the history that brought the patient in, what meds they're on, and so on. I need to know about the patient. Reading medical histories can answer many questions prior to entering a room. Reading progress notes from the doctors also gives great insight to the status of the patient.

There's nothing worse than an uninformed person looking after a patient as sick as the ones we see. If it gets crazy early, then you run the risk of not getting a chance to read the history. If your patient codes, everyone will want to know your patient, including how many kids he has.

So, once that's done, we go in to assess our patients, make sure no fluids are leaking out from anywhere, do the vital signs, and hand out any medications that may be due. Then I like to write my report immediately. If the patient is stable enough, I will bath them, turn, and clean around the bed so the patient can get ready for bed. Again, if the patient is able, we will get him standing as soon as possible, then get them settled for the night. Every hour, we do vital signs and a quick assessment, again looking for a leaky patient. Every two hours we do a group turn. All patients get turned no matter what.

The Game

That's why I like the super sick patients. Many are unable to turn, stand, and so on because they are to hemodynamically unstable. It's not that I'm lazy; it's just not always a priority. If a patient is stable and sleeping, should I wake them, just to turn them? As long as no red spots show up, a patient is okay on her side. It's the elderly that you really need to watch. Nothing is worse than bedsores. In my opinion, bedsores should never happen if you care for the patient and treat the areas of concern.

My patient would not be out for some time, so I helped the others out with the nighttime routines.

Most of the patients were stable. Kind of routine for us on this night. Tonight, in CCU, we had a variety of patients. Mr. James, in room 1, was a sixty-five-year old male who felt the typical left arm pain that radiated to his chest and even into his neck. Luckily, he was at home working in the garden when he became hot and sweaty. He said it was just the sun, but his wife called 911. The paramedics took a twelve-lead ECG and discovered he was in the middle of a heart attack. They gave him two BASA 81 mg to chew and rushed him to our hospital. He was in the Cardiac Cath lab in under an hour, and his distal Left Anterior Descending coronary artery (LAD) was stented.

Mrs. Hanna, a little old lady, was cleaning her house today. She felt pain in her elbow and that was it. So, she finished cleaning, showered, and drove to the emergency department because her elbow was very sore. Many women present with un characteristic pain which often go undetected. Lucky it's routine to hook patients up to a monitor. This monitor showed ST elevation and prompted the RN to perform a

69

twelve-lead ECG. The ECG indicated that Mrs. Hanna's right coronary artery was occluded, causing a right-sided heart attack and providing the reason for her shortness of breath and elbow pain. When we review ECGs or rhythm strips, a normal heart beat looks like a small bump then a big spike and then another small bump. This is an orderly progression of depolarization that starts with our very own pacemaker cells within the heart. This sends a wave through the heart, which is captured as electrical activity. One of the first inventions and major breakthroughs came from Willem Einthoven from the Netherlands. He used a string galvanometer, which is the first practical electrocardiograph that he invented in 1901. Each bump or depolarization is assigned a letter. So, one of the ways we can detect a myocardial infarction is by the elevation of those bumps and spikes. So, the ST elevation is a good indication something is happening with the heart. Depending where those elevations are on the ECG, you can determine which coronary artery might be affected. I loved reading about how or who invented these tools we use each day.

That was the typical patient tonight. This was a good thing, as my patient would take a little monitoring tonight. Good news was the patient would remain heavily sedated tonight to assist in keeping the blood pressure down.

Mr. Jenkins is a forty-five-year-old male who arrived via air ambulance. He was boating and his wife started the boat, which caused him to hit his chest against the dash as he fell forward. Mr. Jenkins thought it was just a bruise until they took him to the Cardiac Cath lab and saw his left coronary artery blocked. He is scheduled for a CABG in the morning.

The Game

Coronary Artery Bypass and grafting is the long version of this. A patient would go into the Cardiac Cath lab to view the coronary arteries. On occasion, the cardiologist is unable to pass a wire through the blockage to open the coronary artery and restore blood flow and oxygen to the affected area of the heart. So, surgery is needed to bypass the blockage. A surgeon will harvest veins from the leg to attach the affected coronary artery. So, the surgeon will sew the vein at the top of the artery and attach the other end to below the blockage. That allows the blood to flow and feed that portion of the heart. Sometimes only one vein is needed to bypass. Other times four or more bypass grafts are required to provide blood flow before the heart muscle is permanently damaged.

Next is a twenty-one-year-old female who tried to OD on mom's cardiac medications. Sally ended up in Premature Atrial contractions (PAT) and just needed to be monitored. So, think of when you run and your heart rate speeds up, sometimes over 120 or more beats per minute. Now think of that going on for about twelve hours straight. Things happen. You become fatigued, short of breath, the amount of oxygen the body uses increases, so your hands and feet can become cold, and organs suffer, and so on. Good news is that being young helps. She will never try that again.

The last patient is Crystal. She is nineteen years old with a two-year-old girl. Crystal was out at a party, took a hit of cocaine, and suffered a massive heart attack. The heart attack was so severe that she needs a heart transplant, just to be able to get out of bed. Her ejection fraction (EF) is less than 35 percent. For now, she keeps telling us she has never touched cocaine in her life.

"I just don't know what happened, someone must have slipped me something in my drink."

"Cocaine is deadly to the heart, not to mention the brain and other organs. Again, feel your pulse on your wrist. That is blood being pumped out of your heart to all parts of your body. Normally our ejection fraction is about 65 percent. That is enough to perfuse all organs and body parts. If the blood is not being pumped out like it should, it builds up and you can go into respiratory complications. If the heart is unable to maintain the blood flow to meet the body's needs, shortness of breath, excessive tiredness, and leg swelling are just a few symptoms." Palmer stated the facts to Crystal.

"So, you'll have no energy to pick up your child, play with her, or even get out of bed." Palmer continued on the rant.

Part of this night is spent talking to both these young girls. Many times, we can sit and chat with patients; they will tell us most anything. After a couple attempts, Crystal finally broke down and started to cry.

"This was the first time I tried it. My friends have taken cocaine several times and nothing happened to them"

"Yes, they were lucky. You had a bad reaction that caused a massive heart attack that will haunt you forever."

"Thanks, Palmer. I need to get my life together for my daughter. She only has me."

"You have your parents, Crystal. Talk to them. You'll probably find out that they will be there for you."

"I will. Thanks again."

"Okay, here is your basin to wash up with. I'll be in later to clean up and let you get some sleep."

The Game

Bev was in Sally's room, telling her that she had been selfish to try this.

"Talk to your mom or get help rather than taking medications to get attention." Even though the door was closed, I knew Bev was all up in Sally's grill. Bev took suicide attempts seriously." I had tried to do the same thing when I was your age." Bev's voice carried out to the main desk.

"Did you like getting your stomach pumped and having to drink charcoal? That's what you will get each time you come in, if you're lucky. I mean if you are alive to get your stomach pumped."

Sally did get her stomach pumped tonight, to neutralize whatever drug she took. She learned a lesson the hard way. Seeing young kids like Sally is why Bev spends time with young girls and talks about what problems or situations they might have.

> "....So injecting protamine sulphate can cause clotting if the blood is thin. If I inject protamine into a person with a stent, clots would form around the stent and close off the artery, causing a heart attack. The package insert says it can cause anaphylactic reactions as well. I think I can do that with no one watching."
>
> Without their precious little accreditation, this hospital will have to listen and promote the good people. You are the brains behind many of our policies, but it's Kerry that takes all the credit. She stole your position, your deserved position. They will pay."

Don McLean

HOW TO PLAY

Many nights are nonstop. Patients coming and going, living or dying through the night. So when it was not busy, we always tried to occupy our time. Unlike some at night, none of us ever slept. We all agreed that it was unprofessional. I remember I tried it one night. I was very tired that night because I had not slept all day. I had just moved into a new house and construction was all around it. This one particular night I put my head down and dozed off. I know now that I was dreaming of a patient calling and I would not answer. That patient died, at least in my dreams. The code blue pager went off, and I woke up - not knowing what was going on and slightly confused. From that night on, I have never slept while on duty. That was ten years ago. Now, I study ECGs, read medical books, or play games. We each take breaks so we can run up and down the stairs or go for a walk just to refresh or recharge the battery in case something comes up. You need to be sharp and ready to roll at a moment's notice. We have seven floors, plus the main floor and the basement. I liked to run up and down the stairs two or three times; then I walk the stairs once or twice. That makes me feel awake and alert, plus when a code was called I was not sucking eggs when I got to a patient's room because I was out of shape. The usual board games were never much fun. So not all of us took part. That's when we started to make up games. One game we played was fun. You picked a medical term out of the medical dictionary, and each player tried to guess what it meant. We had some great answers. A spin-off of that game was another word-centered competition. One player would pick a word and give either the real or bogus definition of it. The other players had to guess which definition was the real meaning. I liked the bogus definitions, because some of them were really inventive.

Our favourite game is just simply called the GAME. The object of the game is simple. How would you kill a patient without anyone else knowing you did it? Could you get away with it, if any one looked at the patient, or if an autopsy was performed? You cannot bring anything into the hospital to help in your crime; you can use only what is typically available on the floor or in the stock cabinet.

At first, it seemed morbid. "How dare we think of ways to do this," Bev would say each time we started, but she joined in anyway.

A simple case example would be a single, large-dose injection of potassium into a patient. The person would go into cardiac arrest and die. If an autopsy was performed, it wouldn't detect the potassium because once a person dies, potassium leaks from the cells into the blood stream, causing a high level of potassium in the blood stream anyway. When a chemistry profile is drawn, it is expected that a high potassium level is seen. The pathologist would not think this result is anything out of the ordinary physical response to death. Cause of death, myocardial infarction. So, the object is for the other players is to determine how one would detect the murder. Katlin was always the one to beat. She knew more than all us.

We never talked about this game outside our own circle. Mostly because not many would understand. The game was like any game, and once it was over, we never talked about it. It was entertaining at the time, but that was it. We have people coming and going all night long. Respiratory techs (RTs), interns, supervisors, cleaning staff, or just other nurses coming in to say hi. All these people thought we were talking about past cases and past patients. We never said it was a game.

I once mentioned the game to another nurse on CSU. I thought Sandra was cool and would do or try most anything once. Before she was married, she did try most everything. She and one of the guys from the same unit were an item. They spent much of their time together, walking each other to Sandra's car after work. One morning, I was late getting out of work. I was walking to the parking lot, and I noticed Ken standing with the car door open and looking down. I waved at him, but he just nodded, like "get lost" as I got closer, I noticed Sandra as well. She was busy, so I went the long way to my car. I don't think she ever saw me, or if she did, she never spoke about that morning.

When I told Sandra that we played the game on occasion, she was upset.

"Hey guys, good evening. What's going on?" Sandra bounced into CCU with her long, raven-black ponytail swishing back and forth.

"We made up a new game, want to play?"

"What kind of game, how do you play it?"

"Okay, you have to think of how you would kill someone without anyone detecting how they died. You can only use hospital equipment, tools, drugs, and so on. No guns, knives, or things like that."

The Game

"How is that a game?" Sandra asked, like we just killed someone. "How can you even think of killing someone who is sick? Did you not see the news not so long ago? A nurse was accused of killing elderly patients with insulin overdose. They arrested her. Is that what you want?" Sandra almost yelled at us as her long, black ponytail swished as she turned and started to storm out.

"Even mad, she still looks great." I have always said.

"Wait, let me explain what we are trying to accomplish. This is our way of learning and teaching each other pharmacology, pharmacokinetics, and the dynamics of medicine we use every day. It's the understanding of pathophysiology."

"I don't want to hear it. It sounds sick. How can you think of killing people? That sounds just like that patient that died of an overdose of insulin. It's not right."

"Oh, come on, Sandra. You never had a patient that you said I wish they were dead under your breath? Palmer questioned, trying to lighten the mood.

I've never told her we still play. When she asks if we play "that stupid game", I just reply no, we play different games.

Not many would understand. It wasn't as if we were going to go out and kill someone, even though there were times we all had thought that one patient would just die.

So, the rules are simple—try to stump the others. You must use drugs, tools, and equipment from within the hospital. We can't use anything from outside the hospital. So, no guns, knives, and so on. We described the situation, the patient, and the way we killed the patient. The more detail the better. If we could add information about the patient's family or loved ones that was even better. The game started simple, but as time went on, our cases became more complicated, more in-depth. Sometimes we saw or heard of a patient die due to some weird cause. We would try to work an angle to use it in our game. Our unit is always busy. Like I mentioned it's a steady flow of respiratory technicians, nursing assistance, interns, and others; every one of them would stop by to talk about the latest occurrence on the floors. It's just something we all did. I think we talked about death, or made jokes about death, so we did not have to deal with the emotional aspect of death. I think when you see people die in front of you day in and day out, it wears on you. Some nurses cry, others laugh, and others just do the job and walk away.

Friends and relatives would ask me about my night and how things went. Did anyone die? They asked this for a long time when I first started. I used to try to explain what happened on the night shift, but it never translated to what really happened. How do you tell someone that you watched a man die, and his family are all around crying and asking why? Most patients are good people, but there are a few that were just mean. But when they die, they look at you like a puppy looks at you, with soft nonjudgmental eyes. It was our job to do everything possible to keep them alive. Even the odd criminal would come in with a heart attack or needing surgery. We don't judge; we just treat and release.

One of the guys who always passed through are unit was Victor Torres. A large, round respiratory technician with just as big a chip on his shoulder as the weight he carried. Victor was in the Gulf War or somewhere like that as a medic. He never really told us where he was situated. He saw a few things that he does not talk about, but all in all he was okay. He complained that either Iran, Iraq, or the USA sprayed them with some sort of chemical, thus his breathing has never been good since his return. Victor was always looking for an angle to get out of work and onto permanent disability. Once you get to know him, it's not bad. But Victor is always negative. He is a good respiratory technician, really knows his work. He runs on codes or at least was at the codes. I was always impressed at how fast he could get to a patient's room. He does use the elevators a lot, but still gets there.

One code we ran on, we both left CCU and by chance the elevator was there, so we both jumped in. The funny thing about that was you are in such a rush, but an elevator only moves so quickly. This night on the elevator, we just stood waiting to rush out the doors. Then out of nowhere we both started to hum the song, "The Girl from Ipanema" – from 1964" It was like the scene from the Blues Brothers where Jake and Elwood were in the elevator and that song was the elevator music. When we arrived at the code and got set up, the ER doc was trying to think of the next step in the algorithm of ACLS. I was doing chest compressions, and Victor was bagging the patient. Which means he was providing 100 percent oxygen. While we waited for the doc to do something, we started to hum our song. Hence my name is Jake and Victor is Elwood, even though Jake was the fatter of the two brothers. It just stuck.

"Hola cómo estás, gringos," Victor always announced as he walked through the doors like a king, depending on his mood.

"Qué pasa, Palmer?"

"Hey, Victor. How's it hanging?"

Victor was a good guy. He fought in the Gulf War, like I said. Actually, he was a medic. When he came back, he had bad asthma and other respiratory problems. All of which the government said they would help with. Which, till this day, they haven't done. Even his own insurance, the same group as he works for now, will not cover the medical problems. Administration says it is a pre-existing disease, and, therefore, it is not covered.

Victor is married to Tara. Tara Ryan is a very pleasant young lady with curly or frizzy auburn hair. Tara is about five foot seven inches tall. She is a hard-working respiratory technician. They both went to the University of Wisconsin-Madison, but they didn't run into one another there. They met while working at St. Mary's Hospital. Both were outgoing and loved walking around Lake Wingra or Henry Vilas Zoo. Although she and Victor moved to town shortly after getting married in Madison, Wisconsin, they didn't both start working immediately. The two seem inseparable, even at work they are always together.

When Victor left for the war, Tara was a wreck. She counted the hours between the face time the two could spend while Victor was away. So, it was probably just short of two years before Tara joined the team. Victor and Tara are in love, I may have said that once or twice.

Victor started working at the hospital as soon as they moved. Tara wanted to wait, get the house set up, and enjoy some downtime.

"Hey, Victor, what's up with you tonight?" Katlin asked.

The Game

"Hey, you guys missed the shift change code, yeah?" He rhetorically questioned all of us.

"What's going on, Victor? You okay, you look out of breath and sweaty?" Barry examined Victor.

"No, man, it's my asthma. It's acting up again. Had to start Prednisone again."

Victor knew that shift change codes are covered by the shift that was on. So, for us, it was always the day staff that went on a code prior to us taking over for the night. We stayed and got report and waited to see if the code would arrive. Then the oncoming nurse would take report from the floor nurse who was bringing the patient in.

"Oh, man, it was great!!" Stacey was elbow deep in the guy's chest.

"Wait, what happened?" Barry asked as he moved closer to Victor.

"Well, this thirty-six-year old guy on SSU was walking around, doing just fine. Kay was with him, walking; laughing, talking, and joking. Next minute, dead. The monitor technician saw a quick run of ventricular tachycardia (VT). Like eight to ten beats, around 180 - 200 bpm and called to the floor to tell Kay what he saw. But by then, Kay had the patient in bed, and he was out."

We had monitor technicians in our unit watching CCU, ICU, and the step-down unit for ICU. The second monitor technician sat in a room, watching the two-step-down units that we shipped our patients to. Their main job was alerting the nursing staff to any problems with the patients on telemetry. Some technicians were very good, and a few not so good.

"So, Ben, the monitor tech on duty, called the unit to ask where the guy was. Like I said, Kay was taking him for a short walk, and they were already back in the room when this happened. Well, he no sooner sat down than he passed out. No pulse, no nothing. Stacey and the code team arrived and started compressions, Dr. Sandoval intubated, and the ICU nurse started a couple of big-ass lines. They called Dr. Beneventi, stat. luckily, she was in post-op and came running."

Dr. Emilia Beneventi is a young redhead with russet-colored hair, gun-metal-blue eyes, gorgeous, and single. She turned every head within fifty feet of her. She looks like one of those super models on a cover of a magazine. She is super nice, dedicated, and one of the best surgeons I have ever seen. The surgical group had been looking for a top surgeon and found Emilia. She was asked to come check out our facilities, and eventually she was hired by the surgical group. Emilia did so well and became such a great surgeon that she eventually took over the heart transplant program, which did amazingly under her watch. The first time I met Emilia was during a code in CCU. She walked in the door and stood beside me.

"Hi, what happened?" Dr. Beneventi questioned Palmer.

"This patient went into respiratory arrest and ventricular fibrillation."

"Oh, did they shock him already?"

"Yeah, this will be the third attempt, and we're getting the amiodarone ready."

"Did they already try epinephrine for this PEA (Pulseless electrical activity)?"

"Yeah, we are getting down to the end of the ACLS algorithm."

"Oh, by the way, my name is Emilia. I'm new to the hospital and just came to watch"

"We just need to stay out of the way, and let the doctor's work." Palmer looked over Emilia.

With surprise on her face, she asked, "Are you not the cardiologist for this patient?"

"Who me?" But I realized she was serious. "Uh, no, I'm just a nurse who started just this week".

"Never say 'just a nurse,' you've told me more about this patient than most interns would."

"Anyway, I thought you were a doctor," Emilia still watched the action.

"Hey, Emilia, get in here and help me out," demanded Dr. Sandoval.

"Well, I've got to go. It was good talking to you. Hey wait, what's your name?"

"Palmer. Hey, Emilia, are you Sandoval's new nurse?" Now it was her turn to laugh.

"No, I'm the new Cardio-Thoracic Surgeon!"

"Then what!" Barry almost peed his pants with excitement.

Victor now got into the story…

"Emilia cut the guy open right there in front of all of us" Victor continued.

The patient already had a sternotomy from his surgery earlier in the week. So, it was no big deal to reopen.

"No way, I'm moving to the day shift, they get all the fun" Barry was now vibrating.

"Hey wait, isn't it odd to walk someone so early after surgery?" Bev was thinking hard about the situation.

"No, he was a couple days post and doing great" Kurt chimed in.

"Dr. Beneventi asked for the rib spreaders and got Stacey to put some gloves on to assist. Dr. Beneventi opens the chest and started to do hand massage on his heart!"

There was no blood flow, so she used her hand to pump the heart."

"She could do a hand massage on me any day" Franco was now wide-awake from the comments Victor was outlining.

"So how did Stacey end up inside the guy's chest" Franco, was now sitting up a little more.

"Dr. Beneventi told Stacey to put the gloves on, while someone poured Povidone-iodine from elbow to hands. Stacey then took a syringe and poked the aorta for blood gases….They were dark as shit! Dr. Beneventi continued to massage the heart, but the guy was dead before his head hit the bed. His aortic root graft blew, and he bled out.

"So where is Stacey now?" Kurt asked, only because he wanted to report and get started.

"Well, she and Emilia are still sewing the guy up, so the family can come in and cry on him without falling into his chest".

Victor finished his report to us with a big grin on his face. "Adiós losers!" as he waddled out the door.

Like I said before, the game also became a way of learning what a medication would do to a patient. How the pharmacokinetics and pharmacodynamics of a medication works. We would learn about pathophysiology, physiological

The Game

complications to a disease, or condition. So, it became a great way to do research. Perhaps that's why our weekend night team were all very intelligent with regard to the pathophysiology of many conditions. I think we all learned a great deal from playing the game as well as working side-by-side with such knowledgeable team members.

To understand where people were coming from, it was always good to know what others did when they were not on the unit. Some of us worked in retirement homes, others flew air ambulance. However, once you knew some of the background, it made it easier to solve the game, because we all used past experiences to try to stump the others.

So, I made it a point to ask what all my teammates did prior to coming to the unit, mostly because we all had another life outside the unit and hearing this made us closer. Not only did it give me an edge on what story each of them would come up with, but we all had interesting past lives. That is to say, what we did prior to nursing or working in CCU.

Katlin, as an example, works with the transplant team at the hospital. She is called whenever a patient is a potential donor. She works hard at calming the family and reassuring them in their time of need. But, she must also ask for organs. Any and all. It helps if a patient comes through the door with a donor card. She can go to the family and say, "this is what he wanted, he signed a donor card to help save lives" Gets them every time.

Her husband, as I mentioned before, is a Physician Assistant. She asks him about pharmacology all the time. The problem as of late, is he is a jerk to her and Meghan.

He is gone for days on end, with very little contact while he is on the road.

What happens when you mix this with that? She used pharmacology in her case scenarios all the time. She always seemed to have the edge on us. I eventually worked on the transplant team and helped in some of our research and protocols for transplants and donors.

"Okay, I have one that we all wish we could do." Katlin gave that sheepish grin that we all had seen on previous occasions.

"Wait, do you think we should keep playing this game given the fact we have had several dead people show up. Oh, and have been killed or died in the same manner we play this game?"

"Well, it's up to you, Bev we don't have to."

"Well, maybe we should review the deaths that have occurred and try to figure something out, added Kurt"

"That's not a bad idea, Kurt."

"Why thanks, Katlin. I do have the occasional enlightenment."

"So, we know that all deaths occurred on nights. That first patient died of a heart attack, or at least that is what the story was. Do you think the killer may have given Potassium to cause a heart attack?"

"Well, that could happen for sure. Again, no way to tell for sure right?" Kurt contemplated the situation.

"Yes, Kurt. That's right."

"Okay, all killed on nights and all by what looks like an undetectable substance. And, all on either step-down units or regular floor units."

The Game

"Yeah, we would've spotted someone from a mile away if it occurred in CCU, ICU, and SICU."

"Correct, Palmer." Katlin looked at Palmer.

"But do you think someone overheard us playing the game, or do you think someone out there has a warped mind?"

"Like us, Bev?"

"Maybe like you, Palmer, but not me. It makes sense someone overheard us, or was told about our game."

"So, Katlin, that includes nurses who come in, respiratory technicians, lab personal, and even the keener interns who stroll in once in a while." Kurt added his comment.

"Okay, but some of the floor nurses said they saw people in scrubs. So, lab technicians are out."

"I think we can exclude critical care nurses."

"Why, Kurt?"

"Well, Silvia said she does not believe it's anyone from ICU. Jared said he does not think SICU staff have anything to do with it."

"Well, that narrows the suspects down. Unless we're lying, Barry."

"Well, we can suspect anyone, but why. What's the motive?"

"Good point, Bev. Why would anyone want to do this?"

"Well, I have talked to Detective Smith a little, and he said…"

"Wait, Katlin, you've been in cahoots with the police?"

"Franco, he came to me and asked if I could keep my eyes open. But honestly I have no clue."

"Whoever it is, they're making us all look bad. We run on these codes, and the patients are dead before we arrive. So, whoever is responsible knows the floor schedules as well."

"I agree, Bev. At least, it's not in the papers. Yet."

"Okay well, let's all keep a look out."

"Yes, ma'am," Franco laughed.

"So, are you going to tell us your next victim, Katlin, or have we stopped the game?"

"Okay, Barry. Let me continue. But I think we need to watch or listen for any patients dying that sound suspicious."

"I agree." Kurt added his two cents.

"These deaths seem to occur almost out of the blue. People are close to going home." Kurt stroked his beard.

"Martha seems to think these patients all are connected. She said they are contributors to the hospital. People with money." Bev recalled Martha's comments.

"Really, is there a connection?" Palmer acknowledged Bev's comments.

"We should ask Mr. Glover next time we see him." Barry looked around at everyone.

"Good call, Barry." Franco jumped in.

"Okay, Katlin. What is your scenario?" Barry seemingly bored with this conversation.

Katlin recounted her tale. "I have a patient coming in who is a potential donor. He has been drinking, so his blood alcohol level is high. He was in a motor vehicle accident and is all messed up. The patient comes in intubated and nonresponsive. The MD starts talking to the family about the patient being a potential donor, as the vital signs are slowly deteriorating. Since I was called to help procure the organs," Katlin continued, "I have to assess the patient. The doctor already has this patient marked as a potential donor. When I enter the room, I notice his eyes twitching."

"Oh, man. This guy's not dead, where are you going with this?" asked Barry impatiently.

"So, as you know we need the organs. Our waiting list is rapidly growing. I go out to the drug cabinet in our unit, and grab the vecuronium bromide. I inject this into the patient's IV and flush with normal saline."

"You paralyzed the bastard." Franco summed up the case so far.

"Yeah, I give a dose of 40 mg of vecuronium bromide IV push, maybe a dose of midazolam as well, and he is not moving or breathing unless he's on the ventilator."

"The doctor comes in to perform the first iced saline injection. As you know, the dead subject will not move when ice water is injected to the ear. The doctor takes him off the vent, continues the brain-dead protocol, and sees no movement. Two hours later, the MD tries the second ice bath and assesses the patient. The patient does not flinch because I have given my second dose of the paralyzer."

"Why do we give a cold-water injection for a potential donor?" Barry asked.

"Well in a normal brain function, we use the cold water, relative to body temperature (30°C or below), the endolymph (fluid in the ear) falls within the semicircular canal, decreasing the rate of vestibular afferent firing. This situation mimics a head turn to the contralateral side. The eyes then turn toward the ipsilateral ear, or same side as the water injection with horizontal nystagmus, or eye movement to the contralateral ear. The vestibulo-ocular reflex (VOR) is a reflex, where activation of the vestibular system causes eye movement. In a brain-dead person, no movement is detected, or doll's eyes. These are just a couple of the tests a doctor will perform in the brain-dead protocol."

"Thanks, Palmer. I get it. We look for anything that would tell us that the patient is still with us. If brain-dead, the patient is dead."

"I got it, wait just one minute," Franco stated all-knowingly.

"The heart is still beating, and he is still breathing. How do you explain that?"

"Well his blood pressure was too low, so we had dopamine running. This will explain a good blood pressure. The breathing only lasts while the patient is on the vent. Since he is paralyzed, he will not breathe on his own, making it look like there is no communication between his brain and his lungs, which will cause him to suffocate when he's taken him off the vent."

"We'll have to account for any of these meds." Bev stated matter of fact.

"True, but these medications are floor stock, and no one really knows how many vials are in the fridge. Pharmacy only adds to the boxes when they see missing meds." Katlin responded in her best lawyer voice.

"I know that may not be the best, but the pharmacy does not expect us to use the drugs for our own good. As you know, when we get patients who are out of control, we will have the doctor order a paralytic. As long as he is already intubated. Therefore, the idea is to be careful that no one watches me draw up any of the meds. If we take the subject off the vent, he becomes acidotic. I need to talk to the doctor to make him believe the subject is dead. You know these guys are always busy and just want us to tell them what is going on."

"So, I get the much-needed organs to help satisfy our waiting list, and we save three or four people by sacrificing one."

"Okay, but that would only be a onetime deal, right?" Kurt asked.

"Why do you say that?"

"Well eventually, someone will wonder why our unit is having such a bad run of deaths, but good fortune in organ procurement."

"True, but I never said we had to keep this only on our unit. What if I carried a small supply around when I get a call to ICU or recovery?"

"Well, that may work," Kurt pondered the situation.

"Wait, you've drawn blood for everything under the sun, including tox screens. You will get caught when the MD sees the paralytic show up on the screen."

"Well, perhaps, but the short-acting medication doesn't leave a trace. Both the paralytic and the anxiolytics are out of the system within an hour. We usually draw blood first before we examine the patient. Plus, why would we look for that in a donor who is not our standard blood draw. ETOH, PCP, and so on. That's what we look for."

"So, we harvest this drunk bastard's eyes, skin, lungs, and lucky for someone, the heart is in good shape. The liver is another thing."

"So, we kill one loser and save several people." Katlin smiled and leaned back in the chair.

"Wow, that is a little too close to the actual work we do," Bev tried to rationalize the actions. "Palmer, keep a close eye on Katlin when you guys work with the transplant team." Bev laughed at her own comment.

"My turn," Franco proclaimed. "A guy is married, treats his wife like shit, drinks all day long, and spends all day out in the yard doing odd jobs, and general puttering around. His wife is the only source of income. She works all day at a restaurant and all night at home, running after him. He barks at her from sun up to sun down. The wife wishes and dreams for a better life. One day, this guy is at home, splitting wood with his log splitter. He too has had enough to drink. While working on the wood splitter, he falls over the machine, and breaks his arm. The guy screams for his wife who is busy in the house."

Franco added as much detail as possible. "She's the glue in the family. He, on the other hand, is the solvent. He drinks, spends all the money, and has no real job. The wife has always said she would be better off if he was dead. Having said that, she still takes care of him, and brings him to the ER. It's late Friday night by the time they get in. Of course, the ER is crazy busy, and that means if you're not bleeding, you need to wait. The longer the guy waits, the more impatient he gets. The guy finally gets called, and the doctor believes his arm is broken but needs an x-ray. Again, waiting for x-rays take forever. The porter finally comes and takes him to the x-ray department. We take x-rays and determine it is a good oblique fracture. Barry, that means it is broken in two" Franco smiled at Barry.

"I know what an oblique fracture is, asshole!"

The Game

"The patient is agitated and wants to go home."

"What's taking them so fucking long!!? Don't they know I'm injured and should look after me?" The guy screams at his wife.

"Meantime, the ER has a few myocardial infarctions and a few more serious traumas. The doc is just too busy to review this guy's chart and set his fracture at this time. So, they give him some morphine and make him as comfortable as possible while he waits."

"Wait, why does he want to leave?" Barry asked.

"The guy is starting to sober up. He is missing his Jack Daniels." Franco continued with his elaborate scenario.

"And, well, let's say I have pissed him off and that he feels he doesn't need to take this crap and is ready to leave. I told him that I would cast his arm so he can go home now, or he can wait until the MD has time, which could be hours. The patient allows me to cast his arm the way it is, without setting it. I cast the arm nice and tight, telling him this will allow the bone to go back to normal. What does he care? He just wants to get back to Jack Daniels and his chair."

"But what does the wife say, Franco?" Kurt now started to think about this.

"I told her to go and sign the 'against medical advice form', as he wants to leave now." Franco continued his description of the story.

"But wouldn't she wonder why his arm is casted?" Kurt now became sceptical.

"No. I told him not to say anything about the cast because the MD will make him stay in the ER until the MD has time to fix him, which will take hours before he can go home. I also tell the patient the technician came in and casted his arm while she was away. I go and get the plaster and quickly cast his arm."

"Okay, but how does he die, Franco?" Katlin queried, now done with her charting.

"I tell him to come back in a few weeks to get the cast cut off. This brings him back to our hospital, and of course, in keeping with our rules, he is set to die in the hospital."

"A broken arm hardly accounts for a death." Bev stated, as she tried to work it out in her head.

"True, so the patient comes into the hospital about five weeks later to get the cast cut off. He comes into the emergency room and states he wants this off. The ER technician takes him to the back and cuts the cast off. The technician asked the patient to wait so we can take an x-ray to make sure all is okay. Well the patient goes to get up from the table and falls over dead. WHY???"

"That's easy. He's drunk, falls, and cracks his head open." Bev stated matter-of-factly.

"No, that is too simple; plus, the alcohol is an outside drug, so we can't use it." Franco fired back

"Okay, Franco. Tell us why" Barry barely contained himself.

"Okay, follow this. The arm was never set, the break formed many fat cells and created a fat embolus to the heart, head, and so on. It traveled from the break straight to the heart, and bang, he's dead." If Franco had had a microphone, he would have dropped it and walked away.

"Wait, how do you know the cast is tight and will cause a fat embolus?" Kurt cross-examined Franco.

The Game

"Well, the break is bad. It's an oblique fracture and must be set to prevent any complications. I merely tell the patient that it will heal on its own. You know very well that most people think a guy in scrubs is a doctor or intern, not a nurse or technician. So, when he comes in and asks for the cast to be taken off, they simply send him back to Roger the technician who will just cut it off. This time, when the patient is asked to sit for a final diagnosis by the doctor, he gets up to walk over to the table, but before he can make it to the table he collapses and dies. The fat embolus has already killed him."

"Wow, that's unbelievable" Barry stated.

"That could work. No one will question you or what you're doing because all the rooms in the ER are private. The wife would be busy while all this is being contrived. The only thing I would have told the wife is to buy life insurance." Bev laughed at the idea.

"Correct, she signed the discharge against medical advice form. The technician could say he was never asked to place the cast and has no documentation of the cast or patient. The wife might try to discover what happened and perhaps the hospital pays her off. She lives happily ever after; she now has no one to beat her up or abuse her anymore." Franco wrapped things up.

"Yeah, and the best thing is, you are not around. So, even if the cops came by, they would only question the ER staff and would not even think to look at you or anyone outside of the ER," Barry recapped the story.

Bing, bing, bing the arrhythmia alarms sound and everyone jumped.

Damien, the monitor tech, explained, "Not us, it's ICU"

"Palmer, start heading down to ICU. I suspect they'll call a code soon." Katlin always had an instinct for this. She was like Radar from the show M.A.S.H. He always knew when the helicopters were coming. Katlin always knew when a code was about to happen.

Katlin sent me because I was a better choice to go into ICU and assist or take over. ICU has many great nurses. This ICU is more medical and not up on all cardiac or surgical complications. Many of my best friends worked in ICU. We in CCU always had fun with ICU. One weekend over Christmas and New Year's Eve, when the patient count was way down, we needed a distraction. One night when Franco and I went to visit ICU and our good buddy Thomas, we came across a toy nurse doll. We asked if we could take the doll upstairs to CCU, but the girls refused. Franco and I kidnapped the doll and held the doll for ransom. We sent a letter, which spelled out our demands, via the pneumatic tube, (a tube system through which you can send letters, samples, and the like to various departments).

"We want six chocolate bars or the doll gets it!!!!"

The ICU replied with a melted chocolate bar wrapped up in a diaper. That was not funny. But it was clever.

You could disassemble this doll without breaking it, so we dislocated the arm and sent a photocopy of the doll without her an arm.

ICU returned the note stating they would not deal with such monsters. This little game went on for a couple of nights; until one night, we came into work and found the doll had been rescued. So we did what had to be done…..

The Game

About 2:30 a.m., Franco and I went to the back door of ICU and snuck in. Kurt and Barry came through the front door. We all carried three or four 60-cc syringes full of water and the big 10-cc instillers that we use for suction, irrigating, and flushing stomach tubes. We went in blasting all syringes and instillers. Well, all the girls ran to the bathrooms and, lucky for us, Thomas was on our side. We captured the doll and returned to CCU with no battle wounds.

However, we underestimated the girls of ICU. At about 0:500 a.m., our doors burst open and there were Silvia, Deb, Linda, and Michelle—each one loaded with five, one-litre enema bags under each arm. They soaked all of us, the unit, the floor, everywhere. It truly looked like a flood. They captured the doll. We never tried that again.

When I arrived at ICU, Deb and Silvia were working on a very big man. He was intubated with a breathing tube and was on a ventilator and had more intravenous lines than a highway map has routes. Silvia came over.

"We are having trouble keeping his pressure up and rhythm stable. I said we should start a central line, which gave better access to the body and will allow us to monitor the hemodynamics of the patient."

"Hey, Silvia, sounds like a good plan." Silvia had already called the intensivist on call, who came up and started the Central Venous pressure line (CVP). We were then able to start an intravenous Inotrope medication to boost his blood pressure. While all this was going on, the patient had ten or fifteen family members waiting to see him. After everything was cleaned up and put away, Silvia let the family in, and the intern went back to CCU. I just opened the doors to CCU and a code blue call came overhead for ICU. I turned and ran back down to the fourth floor.

"What's up down here?" I called as I went back to the same old room.

The code was on the same patient. I arrived in the room and saw all the lines on the floor, Silvia was doing compressions; Victor was venting the subject.

"What the hell is going on," I asked.

"Well…. The family…. Came in…. and … stepped on the lines." Silvia continued pushing down on the patient's chest and explained the situation.

So, we quickly reattached the new IV lines, got the pressure back, and the patient back on the ventilator. All was well for about fifteen minutes.

"When can we go in and see papa?" one of the daughters asked.

"Please, let us stabilize him first," Silvia pled with the family.

"No. Let us go in, he needs us," the daughter cried louder and louder.

The family did not seem to understand the situation and the problem they had caused.

I returned to CCU and sat beside Katlin to fill her in on the excitement in ICU…….

CODE BLUE ICU, CODE BLUE ICU….

"See you in a few minutes." Katlin smiled at me.

This carried on for a few hours, then we finally told the family that with so many people around, the lines would be dislodged because they wanted to hold or touch the patient. Unknowingly, they were the demise of the patient.

Chapter Three

Katlin enjoys days around the house and estate. She will go for walks or ride with Meghan. Today was a little different because Jason was home, and they both are sitting out on the back landing.

"Where were you this week? I tried to call but only got your voicemail."

"I was so busy. I worked and slept."

"Really, what was going on?"

"Not much, just the usual."

"Yeah, I know the usual. What was her name this week?"

"I don't know what you are talking about."

"Jason, stop. I know what's going on. I have seen your phone with all kinds of numbers on it."

"Katlin, I can't take this. Every week, it's the same thing. You know I work hard and am very busy."

"Oh, please. You used to call every day, and now, nothing. When I call you, I either get voice mail or a very short, 'hi, gotta run.' I think it's time for you to spend time somewhere other than here. You upset Meghan and me with your fairy tales."

"What are you saying, Kat?"

"I'm saying you need to leave, leave Meghan and me!" Katlin became agitated and got and paced with anger and frustration.

"Fine, if you want to end this, so be it!"

"You ended this years ago. I'm just making it official. Get out!"

I get up early so I can ease into his day. Today's no different from most. Sipping on coffee, I load up my stereo. I bought this stereo system because of its clarity. I get lost in the moment when it's on. Today Fleetwood Mac was in concert at my house. Not just any album from their amazing repertoire, but the original Fleetwood Mac group, before they crossed the ocean. Fleetwood Mac put out four albums before Stevie Nicks and Lindsey Buckingham joined. As I thumb through my albums, I recall why I purchased this album. I recall the band was founded by guitarist Peter Green, drummer Mick Fleetwood and guitarist Jeremy Spencer. They lacked a permanent bass guitarist for the first few months before Green convinced John McVie to join. That's what I liked most. I searched many vinyl stores to find the album *Albatross*. *Albatross* is a guitar-based instrumental by Fleetwood Mac, released as a single in November 1968, later featured on the compilation albums. This was one of my favorite oldies albums. With such a great music system, and wireless speakers throughout the house, I could kick back anywhere in the house.

The phone rings at Martha's house.

"Hello, Martha. This is Rose. How are you doing?"

"Oh good, Rose. Just taking it easy before our shift."

"Yeah, me too. So, I have some news."

The Game

"Oh, like what?"

"Well. First, we saw those two again in the stairwell, making out."

"Really, I think those two are an item. They come together, then leave together. Probably sleep together." Martha was taking it all in.

"You know Katlin's friend died on the unit today?" Rose reported the story like a news anchor.

"Oh no, that's sad. What happened, Rose?"

"Well, it looks like an allergic reaction. But I think someone planned it. It sounds like the others."

"I told you something is going on. This hospital is killing people," said Martha, her voice now higher than usual.

"I also heard that a detective is looking around at nurses and doctors," Rose added nervously.

"Okay, Rose. I need to go. I have a few things to do before tonight. See you then."

"Okay, Martha. See you later."

SATURDAY NIGHT

Not a good start to the night.

"Did you hear about the code on CSU today?" Martha relayed the news from Rose as she walked into CCU.

"Yes, Martha. We were there running the code." Stacy glared at Martha.

"Does Katlin know yet?"

"Probably not, Martha. She keeps her phone off during the day."

One of the most dreaded phone calls is when it comes from one of your own. Tonight was that night.

First a dear friend and now…….

The Emergency Department called up to CCU.

"Can I speak to the charge nurse?"

"Hi, Sally, sure hold on." Cari the unit clerk putted the caller on hold.

"Hi, Sally. This is Janet. We're almost ready to give report. What's up?"

"We have a thirty-two-year-old male who came in with low heart rate and chest pain. He will need to go to the Cath lab first, but then to you because he might need a pacemaker."

"Okay, that buys us some time. What's his name?"

"His name is Stephen Hughes. He lives here in town. He was at work and started to feel light-headed and some chest pain. He thought he had just been overexerting himself at work."

"Wait, Sally. Does he have next of kin listed?"

"Yeah, his wife, Lisa Hughes."

"Oh no, that's our Lisa from ICU. This is her husband."

The Game

"Oh, man, I am so sorry. I'll let Dr. Bryant know that this guy is one of our own."

I know we should provide care to everyone in the same manner. I also believe the health care profession does just that. When a family member or relative comes into the hospital, things change. Tests are done quicker, things are just completed and reviewed faster. The way I see it, this is our payment for saving lives, helping the sick day in and day out. We never expect any thanks, so when something like this does happen, it's a perk of the job.

"Where's Lisa? Is she coming in?" Sally asked Janet.

"I think she is coming in. I'm not sure that anyone has received word from her yet. Okay, I'll make some calls and track her down."

"Thanks, Sally, talk soon."

"Okay. Let me know if you need anything from me, Janet."

"Hi, Janet. What's going on?" asked Katlin, greeting her colleague who had just hung up the phone.

"Hi, Katlin. Has anyone talked to you today?"

"No. What's up?"

"It's Mary. She coded and died today. I'm so sorry." Janet placed a hand on Katlin.

"Oh my god, I thought she was headed home today. I am going to CSU to see what happened."

"Okay, Katlin, but that's not all."

"What, what else happened?"

We have a patient coming in. It's Lisa's husband."

"Stephen? Where's Lisa?"

"I am about to call the unit now, Katlin. Something tells me she hasn't heard yet."

Janet grabs the phone again and punches in the four-digit number to ICU. Katlin starts to the doors to look at Mary's chart.

"I'll be back in a few minutes, Janet." Katlin motioned toward the doors.

Janet holds her hand over the phone, "Yes, you go. I've got this."

"Hi, Holly. This is Janet. Is Lisa there yet?"

"Hold on, Janet."

"Hello, Lisa speaking."

"Lisa, this is Janet." Janet's voice sounded nervous.

"Janet, how are you? We're just getting ready for report. What's up?"

"Did ER contact you?" Janet still sounded anxious.

"No, are we getting a patient?" Lisa reached for paper to write down the information.

"No, sorry. I mean have they contacted you personally, Lisa?"

"No, what's going on, Janet?"

"Sweetie, its Stephen. He came into ER with a low heart rate and chest pains. He is on his way to the Cath lab."

"Oh, my god. What? When?"

"He'll come to us after he's done, Lisa. Do you want to head down to the Cath lab, and I can meet you after report?"

"Yes, please Janet. I'm heading down now."

"You know that Emerge is great. As soon as they get someone in complaining of chest pain, they get right on it. They don't waste any time – you know all this. Steve is in great hands. Try not to worry too much. I'll see you down there as soon as I can." Janet tried to comfort Lisa.

The Game

"Hi Stephen, I'm Dr. Bryant. We'll be doing things very quickly. Time is muscle is the adage. So, we gave you an ASA tablet to chew. This helps thin the blood slightly and prevents platelet aggregation. We did an ECG and blood work. The blood work helps to show Troponin levels, this is a group of proteins found in skeletal and heart (cardiac) muscle fibers that produce muscular contraction."

"Thanks, Doc. So am I having a heart attack?" Stephen listened intently.

"Yes, we'll give you morphine and nitroglycerin, which help to relax the smooth muscles. I'll open the artery and place a stent. The low heart rate is due to the area of the heart attack. So, the electrical activity of the heart is affected and has slowed the heart rate down. We'll most likely need to give you a pacemaker. I will be back in shortly."

"Thanks Dr. Bryant."

Lisa arrived just as Dr. Bryant finished his explanation.

"Hello, Lisa. Sally mentioned this is your husband and you work in ICU." Dr. Bryant come out of the room as Lisa arrived, nearly out of breath.

"Yes, Dr. Bryant. I came into work and the girls in CCU contacted me and said he was down here."

"Okay. We plan to go in and stent his left anterior descending coronary artery (LAD). The problem with this area, as you know, Lisa, is the amount of damage. The good news is, we prevented a major ischemic event. The bad news is, the area of the blockage knocked out his AV node, and caused a third-degree heart block."

"So, he will need a pacemaker as well?" Lisa recalled her heart anatomy.

"Yes, he has, in all likelihood, sustained extensive damage and will need a pacemaker. Keeping this in mind, let me get in there with your husband and take care of business. The Cath lab has been called and we will go to the lab shortly"

"Thanks, Doctor. Can I go in and see him?"

"Yes, please do."

Dr. Pablo Bryant came from Portugal about three years ago. He's what's called an invasive cardiologist. He is able to perform cardiac catheterization, stents, and implant pacemakers. In some countries, like Canada, the pacemaker is implanted in the operating room by the thoracic surgeon. Many cardiologists can implant a pacemaker very easily with little to no problems post insertion. Dr. Bryant was recruited by the hospital because of his skill in opening arteries and stenting. His success rate is through the roof and complications are less than 1 percent.

"Hi, babe, how are you?" Lisa eyed the heart monitor and the IV lines running to her husband's arm.

"I feel better now that they gave me morphine. This is great stuff."

"You're in good hands with the team here. Thank goodness you got here as soon as you did."

"Hi, Stephen. We are here to take you up to the Cardiac Cath lab." John came through the door with a stretcher.

Stephen is ushered to the Cath lab with Lisa at his side.

"We'll get him set up, are you coming in to watch?" John asked, as they opened the doors to the Cath lab.

"No, I'm not sure I want to watch. I'll wait. Janet is coming down from CCU."

"Okay, we will be out soon to talk."

The Game

"Lisa, how are you? Is Stephen in the lab?"

"Janet, thanks for coming down. Yes, they just took him in. You know when this happens to a stranger, you can sit and comfort them and say it will be okay. But being on this side, sucks. I'll need to rethink how I talk to family members."

"That's funny, Lisa. It makes us more aware, for sure. Did Pablo say he'll come out and talk to you?"

"Yeah, they're opening his LAD first and then going to put a pacemaker in later. The pacemaker may wait until Stephen has rested for a day or so." Lisa relayed Dr. Bryant's words.

"Yeah, we can put an external pacemaker on, or Pablo may insert a temporary pacemaker, which will buy time for Stephen to rest."

"Katlin will take Stephen, and watch him tonight. If you want to stay or come and go, that's not a problem."

"Thanks, Janet. I need to check in on ICU. We are good staff-wise, and we don't have too many patients."

"Well, that's good timing." Janet smiled.

"Stephen has always been one for timing," Lisa quipped, and both nurses laughed.

"I'll run up to the unit, check in, and, if possible, come back or meet Stephen in CCU." Lisa started to stand up.

"Okay, I will wait here until they come out. I can walk him upstairs before I go." Janet also stood with Lisa.

"Thanks again, dear. You've been a big help."

"No problem, Lisa. Cheers."

"Hi, Mr. Glover. Thanks for allowing me to come in and look around."

"No problem, Mr. Smith, I mean detective. We want to cooperate with the police and allow you access as needed. Besides administration called and has cleared it for you to come in."

"Great! Can we take a tour of the hospital? I want to see the floors those deaths occurred on."

"Sure, let's start down here in the basement and work our way up."

"Do you know Martha Newsome, Mr. Glover?"

"Oh yeah, who doesn't? Martha is our resident expert on all things going on in the hospital."

"What can you tell me about her?"

"Martha is harmless, unless she decides to talk or gossip about you. She has a little information and will fill in the details with her imagination. She lives alone, but has a couple partners in crime, if you get what I mean."

"She called me a while back, stating that she believed a nurse or doctor was actually killing people in the hospital. This was almost the same time that Brooks called me about these patients. How do you think she knew this?"

"Good question, Smith."

"Well, I do manage to get some wood on the occasional ball." Mr. Smith laughed quietly.

"I think there might be some others who have thought something untoward was happening to patients. People talk. So, I can only assume that Martha got wind of somebody else's speculation and ran with her conspiracy theory."

"Okay, who are her partners in crime, as you say?"

"I believe they would be Rose Flowers, and Ruth McGovern."

"Seriously, Flowers?"

"Yeah, her parents must have liked flowers."

"Let me show you a couple things. We have many stairwells that take you to all units. This stairwell takes you from the top to the bottom of the hospital. The other stairs down that hall go up to the fifth floor only."

"Okay, so you can take one set and cross over to another set of stairs without anyone seeing you, correct?" Smith was getting the layout in his head.

"Yes, you can hide in many places in the hospital if you want to."

"Okay, let's go upstairs, Glover. While we're on our tour, can we talk to Martha?"

"Yes, she should be starting her shift."

Glover takes Smith over to the elevators and up to CSU where Martha is working tonight.

"How many deaths that the hospital believes are in question have there been?" queried Smith as he looked down at his ever-present book.

"Well, if you count the one that occurred today, I think four." Glover looked up at the numbers rolling by.

"Does anyone have an idea of who may be killing these patients?"

"No nothing of substance, Mr. Smith. Some people seem to think it has to do with some of our sponsors that have donated money or have some sort of connection to administration."

"Has administration confirmed this?" Smith now looked up at the numbers at the top of the elevator door.

"Yes, our CEO indicated the three are contributors, and this last murder, I mean death, is a friend of a nurse." Glover looked down at the floor.

"Here we are, Mr. Smith, I mean Detective Smith. Let's take a right. The report room is just around this corner."

"The patient in 728 bed two is doing well. They will probably discharge tomorrow."

"Okay, thanks, Jen. I'll keep an eye on her, sounds like a quite night."

Glover and Smith turn the corner, just in time to see Martha.

"Here is the report room, Mr. Smith, let's see if Martha has time."

"Hi, Martha, are you free?" Mr. Glover peeked around the door.

"Yes, Mr. Glover. Jen and I just finished."

"Martha, this is Mr. Smith, ah, Detective Smith. He has a few questions for you."

"Oh, yes. Hello, detective, how can I assist you?"

"Well, were you the one who called Police Headquarters the other day?"

"Yes. I thought the authorities should be aware of the murders that have been taking place at the hospital. The administration is doing nothing, so I thought it my duty to call."

"I'm glad you did." Smith half smiled at Glover. "What can you tell me about these murders, you called them?" Smith reviewed his notes.

The Game

"We have had several unexplainable deaths in the hospital. My friends on the other floors have all confided in me. They can't explain the deaths."

"Who are your friends?" Smith was taking notes.

"Rose, Rose Flowers and Ruth McGowan."

"Who do you think is doing this, Martha?" Smith didn't look up from his notebook.

"Well, clearly a nurse or doctor is doing this. But he is not alone. I think there is a second person."

"Why a nurse or doctor, Martha?"

"Well, these deaths are suspicious. The medical examiner doesn't know how they died. But the deaths are meant to look like heart attacks and respiratory distress."

"Okay, so did you see anyone try to commit these murders?"

"No, but I know those night nurses in CCU play a game that is designed to kill someone without being detected. I think they might know."

"Oh, how so?" Smith looked directly at Martha.

"They come up with a situation to try to stump the others. Like giving a diabetic an overdose of insulin. No one would see you do it, and it goes undetected."

"Well it seems you know how to kill someone as well. Did you know the one patient died of an insulin overdose, or are you just stating it as a for instance?"

"I overheard a doctor mention the overdose while he was on the phone."

"Which doctor?" Smith still stared at Martha.

"Not sure, he was short, old, grey hair. Had some sort of backwoods accent."

Smith looked at Glover as they both said, "Brooks" and laughed.

"Okay, we will talk to the doctor. Is there anything else, Martha?"

"No, but I would talk to that CCU group."

"I see. One more question, do you play this game?"

"Oh, heavens no, that is just wrong. Plus, they only seem to play the game when no one else is around. I have walked in on them, and they all stop talking. Like they are hiding something"

"Who does?" Now Glover stepped up to Martha.

"Well, it's all the weekend night crew. Katlin, Palmer, Barry, Franco, and Bev."

"Anyone else?" Smith looked at Glover to back up the information.

"No. They don't like to discuss this game with anyone they consider an outsider. It's like a big secret."

"But others might walk in and overhear them, right?" Smith shot questions at Martha.

"Yes, that could be nearly anyone from linen attendants to doctors." Martha flipped her hand like she was shooing a fly.

"Okay, thank-you, Martha. I will contact you if I have any more questions."

"Okay, detective. I'm here to help!" Martha picked up her chart and walked to her patient's room.

"Okay, Glover, do you know these two other persons Martha mentioned? I would like to talk to them."

"Yes, Rose is on the fifth floor. I believe she is on tonight. Ruth is on the sixth floor, but I'm not sure what her schedule is. We can check."

The Game

"Did you learn anything, detective?"

"Oh, yes. Not to talk to her again." Smith smiled at his own comment. "No, actually, she was most helpful. It sounds like the murderer might be using this game to hide behind. It's probably someone who does have access to CCU and has heard this game being played."

"Great, let's go back the way we came. We can take the stairs down one floor." Glover pointed back over Smith's shoulder.

Once Saturday and Sunday hit, things calm down. No surgeries are scheduled unless it is an urgent case, and the same with the Cardiac Cath labs. That makes these nights more relaxing. We can train new nurses on these nights because we have more time to review. When the heat is on, it is difficult to explain why we are doing things. We just do them, and then when we have time we can review with the new person. This night was not like that. It was busy.

Report went quickly; we had only seven patients in the unit. Stephen will up the count to eight patients. But once he's stabilized, he will be fine. We have four open beds, but only two that we would fill from the ER.

"Well, good evening, Palmer. How are you and Katlin doin'?" Martha smirked at Palmer as Palmer walked into the unit.

"I'm fine, Martha. You'll have to ask Katlin how she is." Palmer looked a little annoyed, reading Martha's snide remark correctly.

"Oh, did Katlin not come in with you? I thought you guys' carpooled." Martha tried to scoop some juicy tidbits for her fellow gossipmongers.

"Bye Martha, I'm going for coffee. I could use some." Palmer changed topics.

"Hi, guys." Bev was also looking for the coffee.

The others arrived and got settled for report.

After the group report, we headed out to talk to the day shift. The day shift always thought they were better than us on nights. There was always a theory that day shift was the better and had more skilled nurses.

"Only the lazy or not so smart work nights!!" Is what they say. Well, I would take any one of our team members and many other nurses on nights over the day staff. We were alone on nights, no doctors roaming the units, no one to lean on. Yes, we can call the intensivists or the doctors on call. But they expect us to think things through. Why wake a doctor for an order for Tylenol when we can give two and ask for the order in the morning. Doctors expected us to always think. That's what sets the critical care nurse apart from non-registered nurses. That ability to think critically and process.

Today Mary was set to go home. Somehow when the nurse checked labs, they detected the partial thromboplastin time, a blood test that looks at how long it takes for blood to clot. Normal ranges vary between twenty-five to thirty seconds. Mary's PTT was twice normal. The nurse called the intern to come review the case.

"Hi, I am doctor Moya. What's going on?" Kara, the floor Nurse, showed Dr. Moya the lab results.

"She is to be discharged today, but I thought I would ask about this lab result."

The Game

The intern instantly insisted, "Get me protamine sulfate, IV now please, protamine sulfate will reverse the effects of heparin.

"They said Mary looked blue almost as soon as he gave the medication," Cheryl continued.

"Did they not check her chart?" Katlin was red eyed and looked at Cheryl for an answer.

"I guess not, why?" Cheryl questioned.

"Mary was allergic to shell fish. Anyone who has an allergy to shell fish should not receive protamine. Plus, why would they give protamine with no heparin running?"

"Oh my, Katlin, that is just not right. I don't know what happened other than the intern insisted on giving the drug." Cheryl looked at her notes and back at Katlin.

"When did this happen?" Katlin followed up.

"I think earlier today, just before shift change. It was nuts here. Mary's code was called at the same time ER called telling us about Stephen. So, Janet went to the Cath lab; Karen ran on the code. Katlin, I am so sorry about your friend. Do you want to go home or be with the husband?" Cheryl summarized the day's events.

"No, I am fine."

"Katlin, why not go home and relax. Talk to her husband, do whatever. I can run things here tonight." Palmer held Katlin around the shoulders for support.

"No, I want to be here. I might go look at the chart later tonight."

"Okay, let's get the report over with, and you and I will go for a walk." Palmer still held Katlin.

"Where's Janet?" Katlin looked around.

115

"She is still down with Lisa's husband and Lisa." Cheryl looked at Katlin.

"Oh yeah, you said that already. Okay, I will take Stephen when he arrives."

"That would be great. I know you and Lisa are also close." Cheryl's eyes were red with unshed tears as she watched Katlin sit down for report, which is usually loud and mostly a happy time, was not that way tonight. News traveled quickly about Mary. So, report was solemn.

I'm assigned one patient. Mr. Boivin. He had a previous myocardial infarct and was back in because of a new MI, but he ended up in surgery for a Mitral Valve (MV) repair and a two-vessel bypass.

The repairs to Mr. Boivin's heart will alleviate his issues with shortness of breath, heart palpitations, dizziness, and other uncomfortable, and potentially fatal, complications. The surgery will restore his heart so the mitral valve works properly, allowing the blood to flow from the left atrium chamber to the left ventricle without any of the blood flowing back into the left atrium. It was definitely a serious condition and surgery was needed, but Mr. Boivin's large family was concerned beyond all the norms.

I completed my usual assessments; reviewed the entire chart prior to entering the room and reviewed Mr. Bovin's medications. Because he is vented and sedated, he will need to be quiet for twenty-four hours, mostly to let the myocardial infarction subside and let the mitral valve heal. Once in the room, I always check the patient's airway and breathing and the ventilator settings, like the fraction of inspired oxygen (FIO2), which is the fraction or percentage of oxygen

The Game

in the volume being measured. Patients who experience difficulty breathing are provided oxygen-enriched air, which means a higher than atmospheric FIO2. If a patient requires a higher FIO2, this could be an indication of hypoxemia. Mr. Bovin was sedated, so his values were within normal limits. When a patient is sedated, we can provide the rate that the ventilator provides a breath, so, as the patient wakes up, the ventilator will allow the patient to initiate their breath. Next, I checked the circulation to make sure I could hear heart sounds, like a heart murmur or any signs that might indicate a faulty valve. Then, in characteristic thoroughness, I reviewed Bovin's blood pressure, pulse, rhythm, and abdominal sounds, to make sure his bowels were working. I felt for leg pulses and urine output. Finally, I made sure all the IV drips were correct. The goal is to optimize the IV drips and fluids for the best cardiac output. Once all the checks were done, I wrote my report and made sure the patient was sedated and comfortable.

After I wrote up my first report on the patient, I gathered Mr. Bovin's family members together in the patient's room. This is the best place to review the patient's status. "Mr. Bovin is resting comfortably after his surgery, but I'm sure you understand that his condition is serious, and he'll need to rest for some time."

"If he is so stable, how come he's on a ventilator and all those IV medications?" Jennifer is Mr. Bovin's youngest daughter, but she's eighteen years old.

"Good question, Jennifer. Your dad is stable. We take everything into consideration. His blood pressure and heart rate are both good. So that helps us understand he is relaxed. He is on the ventilator to allow proper oxygenation. If we let him breath on his own, he might not take in the adequate amount of oxygen. That could cause problems, like pneumonia. He is sedated, because let's face it, who wants to be awake and breathing through a tube? So basically, we are letting him rest, and recover. In the next day or so, we will get rid of the ventilator, decrease and stop most of the IVs, and get rid of those chest tubes."

Mr. Boivin is an important man in the state. He owns a business at the local resort. He and his family have built the business and the town up to what it is today. Everyone has gone to his restaurant every summer probably since they were kids.

Katlin is in the room with Stephen and Lisa. Stephen arrived and is all tucked into bed. Dr. Bryant left the arterial line in place as a precaution.

"Lisa, as you know, Stephen will be flat on his back most likely overnight. Just as well. He was given lots of morphine and Versed in the Cath lab."

"Yeah, that's fine. He loves sleeping on his back."

"All his vital signs are stable; he is doing well. The temporary pacemaker will help if his heart rate drops."

"Thanks, Katlin. Dr. Bryant explained everything to me. I may go home later. Katlin, I heard the others talking about your friend. I am so sorry."

"Thanks, Lisa. You have your hands full as well. Call if you need anything. We'll keep Steve sedated, so you'll be able to go home."

"Hey, Palmer. Are you ready for a break? I have Steve quiet and stable."

The Game

"Yeah, Kat, let's go now. I will need to be back soon to check on my guy. The family is just leaving."

"Before you go, has anyone given more thought about these deaths or murders?" Barry pondered the events.

"A little, Barry. My friend died today, and there is no reason as to why."

"So, someone is definitely killing people. But why?" Barry looked around the unit.

"Well, when last I talked to Smith, he mentioned all these people have something in common. They are all rich or contributors to the hospital."

"When did you talk to the detective, Katlin?" Bev looked puzzled.

"I went to see Mary, and I ran into Detective Smith. We talked about a few things."

"Were Mary and her husband rich?"

"No, Bev. That's what makes no sense. They did volunteering, but that was about it."

"Yeah, but she knew you. So, does someone have something against you, Katlin?"

"Maybe, Kurt, or perhaps her death is just to make a point."

"Like what? The killer can attack anyone?" Kurt was troubled as well.

"But it sounds like the other patients had something to do with the hospital. So, is someone sending a message to the hospital administrators?"

"Possible, Barry. But why?" Bev sat at the table.

"Well, I know many of my friends are upset with no raise, poor equipment, and lack of real benefits for our healthcare."

"But Barry, do you really think someone is willing to kill so we can all get a pay raise or new equipment?" Kurt stood over Barry.

"Well, it doesn't make sense. But killing doesn't make sense." Katlin added her comments.

"Well, it does seem that the killer has time to set up these murders and complete them before anyone detects them. Could it be someone who is familiar with every floor and knows a little about medications?"

"Perhaps, Palmer." Katlin looked at him with slightly reddened eyes thinking of her dear friend.

"Well take that one lady who got super sick after they discovered that she had ingested her eye drops. Do you think that was on purpose, or does the killer watch too much TV?"

"Right," Bev chimed in, "I think that was a mistake. I think the killer thought it would kill her."

"Did that patient identify the person who gave her the eye drops?" Kurt questioned the group.

"No, she said she didn't get a good look at the nurse because it was dark."

"But it was a female, Palmer?"

"I guess. The patient thought it was a female."

"Okay, all of us guys are off the hook." Franco laughed as he moved to his rooms.

"Okay, I'm going to take a break. I'll be looking at Mary's chart."

"Sure, Katlin, let's go have a look."

"Okay, Palmer. Let's go to see my friend's chart, okay?"

We liked to stroll through the hospital now and then, just to get away from all the others. Don't get me wrong, we liked our team and got along with everyone very well. But sometimes, we wanted to talk about things that we didn't want the others to overhear. So, we went for a walk Today was different; we had a purpose—Katlin's friend.

"How are you really, Kat?" asked Palmer, as he and Katlin walked out the doors to the nurse's desk to look through the charts.

"I'm okay, just frustrated by what happened. Things don't add up. I need to call her husband when I can."

Katlin is an amazing woman. She works hard and is well respected. We enjoyed being together. We spent time at work and off work. We can relax around each other, tell our secrets and ambitions. Our talks range from family to doctors to who is doing whom.

"How are things at home, Kat." I tried to change topics while we walked to the floor.

"He's pissing me off again." Katlin started up as if we had never stopped talking about him from the last time we went for a walk.

"Why, what's up now?"

"I think he has a nurse on the side, actually I know he does, He has been calling and telling me it's too late to come home, and he stays at a hotel. One night turns into two nights and now it's three nights. Nowadays, if I call him, I either get a voice mail or a short, gotta run call."

"Wow, does he think he's fooling you?"

"Well, he must, because he says nothing's going on," she added, as we walked down to the second floor of the hospital.

"His phone was left on the end table the other night. I looked at it, and he had several phone calls from a number that is not from the hospital. When I asked him about it, he just said the physicians called him"

"That could be true," Palmer played the devil's advocate.

"Well, yes, only the MD doesn't call six times after 10:00 p.m. I am done with him. I need out of my life. So, I told him to leave."

"Wow, good for you." Palmer commented.

"Hi, Carly. Can I see Mary's chart?" Katlin wasted no time on small talk.

"Oh, Katlin. I'm so sorry. I know she was a dear friend. Yes, let me get it for you." Carly walked toward the charts. "I have it right here. A detective came to look at it. He wanted to make some copies, but I told him we need administration's approval."

"Oh, he's quick." Katlin reached to get the chart from Carly.

"What time did all this happen, Carly?"

"Looks like toward the end of the day. The labs came back, and we were ready to discharge her. But then Marnie saw the elevated PTT and thought she should call the intern before discharge."

"Thanks, Carly."

"Sure, Katlin, let me know if I can help."

"Did anyone call you or notify you?" Palmer sat next to Katlin and looked over her shoulder.

"No, Bob probably had too much going on to think about calling me."

"Look, Palmer. The admission page clearly shows an allergy to shellfish, but that information did not get carried over from that page to any MD progress notes."

"That seems odd. We always transfer the allergies from one page to the next, so everyone is aware of them."

"Look at these labs. The PTT is normal every day, except for today," Katlin flipped through the chart.

"It's as if someone gave her a dose of heparin." Palmer read the lab results.

"Yeah, look at these times. The lab is drawn at 4:00 PM., the results were called to the intern at 6:00 PM. and the protamine is given at 6:30 PM." Katlin grabbed Palmer's arm in shock. "But look, there was no order to give protamine."

"Carly, do you have the order for protamine?"

"Yeah, the intern wrote it out. It's here in the in box."

"Can I see it?" Katlin inspected the order that Carly handed to her.

"Look, the order reads 50 mg IV push." That's way too much. How did no one pick it up?"

"Could it have been an error?"

"Hard to say, Palmer. You would hope that lab results are accurate, and the order as well."

"Look at the nurse's comments. She mentions an allergy, but the intern gave the protamine anyway, then wrote ready for discharge."

"Yeah, and a code was called at 6:45 PM." Palmer reviewed the code page.

"She deteriorated quickly, Kat. I'm so sorry."

"But look, there's no record of heparin ever having been given, and why would anyone give heparin? She was on clopidogrel already." Katlin's questions continued to build.

"Look at the order, Kat. Do you see anything funny?"

"Protamine Sulphate 5 0 mg IV push – Dr. Moya"

"Wait, that looks like the zero was added." Katlin looked at the back side of the order form. "Yeah, look Palmer, the writing does look different."

"This is making my Spidey sense crawl," Palmer agreed with Katlin that something wasn't adding up in her friend's death. It seemed so unlikely that the hospital's well-known and observed protocol had failed.

"This is not over. I need to take some time to look it over. But tonight is not the time. I can't spend all night out here. I need to go back and see how Steve is doing."

"Okay, Kat. We can come back."

As we reached bottom of the stairs that would take us back to CCU, Katlin had a look of disbelief on her face. Stopping, Katlin asserted, "Palmer, something is wrong. This is just wrong." She started to cry.

Palmer put his arms around Katlin, and she did not resist. She hung unto him like her life depended on him as they just stood together.

"Thanks, Palmer, I needed a big hug. I'm glad you are here holding me, but we should go. I saw Rose snooping around earlier, and I am sure we are already on the hot wire."

"I'm not sure what to say, but I agree. We need to look into this, or at least ask more questions," Palmer responded as he locked eyes with Katlin. He was aware that his words could be construed to mean something other than concern about the death of Katlin's friend. But they had been away from the floor long enough, and they needed some exercise before they went back to work. As they started up the stairs, Palmer asked, "What's your plan now, Katlin?"

"This is not over." Katlin took two stairs at a time.

"Between this and your husband, it has not been a good week."

"I told him to leave. I need some time and space. He left without too much complaining." Katlin instantly changed gears as we both got ready to focus on work. "Meghan and I will do just fine. She also thinks he is up to something. He has not been honest with me or Meghan." Katlin finished her thought. "Maybe I should find someone that I enjoy being with. Someone who's easy to talk to. I seem to be able to tell you about anything. Thanks for that."

"No problem, that's why I'm here."

"Did you hear that?" Katlin grabbed Palmer's arm to head up the stairs.

We hit the top of the stairwell and decided to go one more lap. This time down and back up, we lightened the talk and mood was more fun. We joked and laughed at a few of the gossip stories that we had overheard this weekend.

We had just arrived back at CCU, laughing about the idea, when the code blue sounded.

CODE BLUE, SECOND FLOOR, CODE BLUE SECOND FLOOR.

We are certified yearly for Advanced Cardiac Life Support, Pediatric Advanced Life Support, and Trauma. The reviews or training for all of these certifications is long. Recertification is not as lengthy, as long as you know what to do. If not, the doctor who is recertifying us will question us over and over until we get it or fail and need to recertify again later. One night, I had a lengthy code that lasted over an hour. By the time we were done, I had no chance to study for my recertification the next morning. The doctor who was performing the re certifications asked how my night was. I explained the entire code to him.

He said, "Sometimes no matter what we do, patients still die." The doctor did several re certifications and was very hard on the nurses. He expected us all to perform at a high level. He expected us to anticipate the next move and next step. When it came time for my recert, the doctor restated the scenario I had just told him.

I laughed and said "Call the code because the patient died."

He laughed and made me relive the code. The other nurses could not believe what he was asking me for, but he and I knew what the scenario was about. I passed.

"I have this one," said Kurt. "It is my turn tonight, and Silvia is running codes for ICU."

Kurt and Silvia liked doing codes together. It gave them a chance to see each other during the night.

The code was quick and simple. The patient was recovering from a heart attack and PCI. He was due to go home in the morning. When the team arrived to 2 a, Kurt hooked him up to the defibrillator, and just a flat line appeared. Dr. Sturgeon intubated the patient and asked Silvia to started CPR. Kurt tried to shock the patient because the rhythm was a fine VF. June from the ER, gave Epinephrine, but nothing happened. Victor was there to assist in intubation. Kurt drew ABGs and a potassium level. Dr. Sturgeon continued the ACLS protocol, but not with much gusto. Sometimes, you just know when the patient is heading to the light.

It is tough for the floor nurses to watch this go on because they get close to the patients on this floor. Patients often come back to see the nursing staff. The nurses sometimes feel we did not do enough to get the patient back. But that is life on a code. Fewer than 30 percent of patients come back from coding. Fewer than 10 percent will actually walk out the door.

"Shouldn't we be doing more?" Shelby asked, looking down at the patient and back at Dr. Sturgeon.

"Sorry, Shelby," Dr. Sturgeon replied. "This guy was dead before we ever got here."

"We don't normally check patients on the hour, but rather every four hours." Shelby stated to no one in particular. "This is routine on this floor. A stable patient should not need much follow up. Just a good-night. So, this guy might have coded some time ago, and we didn't know."

The blood gases came back extremely acidotic, and the potassium level was very high—7.5," Dr. Sturgeon stated. "This is not uncommon if the patient was dead for a while because the potassium level tends to leave the cells and enter the bloodstream, looking like a huge bolus of potassium level was given. But we know that would never happen. Sometimes, it is just their time, Shelby."

The team cleaned things up, and the supervisor made the call to the family. This would be a shock. There had been no indication that this patient was in distress.

"I thought all was okay after I saw two nurses leave the room earlier this evening." Shelby stated to the supervisor. "Should I be available to answer questions?"

"Yes, Shelby. I might have a question or two for you." Richard looked at Shelby to make sure she was okay. Mr.

Smith was standing out of the way, but taking it all in. Smith still shadowed Glover around the hospital.

Once the action was over, Kurt and Silvia returned to CCU. They both came in to CCU and sat down to explain what had happened. After they revealed the events, Katlin looked at them and Palmer, as she stated, "Well that was a kind of uneventful code. I want the next one that comes by. It should be way more exciting than this last one." Kurt shook his head.

Having exhausted the excuse for being with Kurt, Silvia declared, "Well, I need to get back to ICU."

Kurt got up to walk Silvia back to ICU...... he was gone for about forty-five minutes before he returned to his patients.

He never did get another code that night. What was great for the patients, wasn't so good for Kurt. He got bored, which made the time pass slowly. Don't get me wrong, we all wish the best for all patients. But when a code is called, that is the time we most enjoy. We want to be the ones to help save that patient.

Richard Glover was an ex-nurse, turned night supervisor. He was a cool person. He understood the needs of the hospital and the reality of nursing staff and workloads. He was quick to jump in and always stood up for the staff. If he could call extra staff in when needed, he did it.

"Hey, Shelby. Have a minute to talk about what happened?"

"Yeah, Richard. I have a few minutes before the family comes in."

"This is Mr. Smith. He is a detective who is following me around tonight. You mentioned that you saw two nurses

The Game

leaving the room before this code. Do you know who they were?"

"Hello, Mr. Smith. No. I didn't get a good look. One was tall and one a little shorter. Both had scrubs on, like they were CCU, ICU or….."

"Or what, Shelby?" Smith probed.

"Ah, respiratory technicians. They wear scrubs. It could have been them or anyone. Richard, isn't that right?"

"Yes, they do, Shelby."

"Okay, thanks. Please let Mr. Glover know if you think of anything else." Smith flipped his notebook closed and placed it into his breast pocket.

"Will do." Shelby was now in a better mood.

"Will Brooks be looking at this patient, Richard?" Smith started to walk.

"Yeah, he will probably want to do an autopsy in the morning."

"Okay, I may want to talk to Brooks after he's done."

"Sure, I can ask him to keep us informed." Glover now made a note to talk to Dr. Brooks.

"Thanks, Richard. Does anyone ever live to go home?"

"Well, yes, but when someone codes, the statistics are grim. The percentage of people who recover from a code is slim."

"Also, it makes sure no one talks, if they're dead."

"I suppose, detective."

"I heard someone say the potassium levels were high. Could someone have given an overdose of potassium to cause this?"

"Perhaps, but that is such a scary idea, I don't want to even think of that."

"In my line of work, I don't rule out any possibility. People do things that make your hair stand up on end."

"Let's finish up here, and I can take you through the rest of the hospital."

"Thanks that would be helpful, Richard."

CHAPTER FOUR

SUNDAY NIGHT—LAST NIGHT FOR A FEW DAYS…

Usually by Sunday, the hospital has tried to move patients out or down to the step-down units. The more beds the hospital can fill in the coming week the better because the hospital generates its revenue by filling beds. Insurance plays a big role in revenue. Hospitals can bill for patient stays for everything from a water bottle to a bandage. IV pumps are billed like renting a TV from the candy stripers. Each IV pump is billed. In order to maintain its certifications, this hospital also must take in many non-paying patients. This is one of the reasons I like this hospital. We take everyone and do not turn them away. I have been to hospitals where, if you did not have insurance, you were transferred to a city hospital.

"Hi, Mr. Glover. Thanks for letting me come in tonight. I had a few follow up questions. Can we go to CCU?"

"Sure. Again, it is no problem taking you on the tour." Glover smiled as they headed up to CCU.

"Hey, Mr. Glover. How goes the battle?" Katlin made conversation.

"Good, Katlin. How are things here?"

"It's early, but all is good. What brings you by?"

"I want you to meet Mr. Smith, Detective Smith—sorry John."

"Well, had I known you were bringing a guest, I would have dressed up." Katlin smiled at Smith. We have already met Richard."

"Hi Ms.?" Smith trying to recall if he had asked for a last name.

"Call me Katlin, detective. What's going on?"

"I want to talk to your staff before you start your shift. I have a few questions about the death of a few patients in the hospital lately."

"Okay, shoot. Oh wait, that's probably not the thing to say to a cop."

"You were around last night too, right?" Mr. Smith took out his little black book and opened it to the middle. "Can you tell me where you were last Friday?"

"Here, like always."

"I hear you take walks and travel through the hospital. That's convenient! I mean to have the freedom to move from floor to floor undetected. Do you walk through the hospital every night?"

"Well, if it's not busy, yes. We all do." Katlin answered Smith's question, while looking at her watch and twisting it around her wrist. "Who has been telling you stories, Mr. Smith?" Katlin stared at Smith with a blank expression.

"Have you seen any suspicious people roaming the halls?" Smith ignored Katlin's question.

"No, just the usual nuts—nurses, respiratory technicians, doctors, security, police detectives."

"Anyone who should not be where their assigned to."

"Again, no detective. We all have access to the hospital; it's not uncommon for staff to go for walks. It's more uncommon not to see staff walking around. Do you think someone is knocking off patients?" Katlin now tried to investigate Smith's concerns and turn the table around on him.

"Well, it does seem odd that this hospital has more deaths with unknown cause than any of the other hospitals in the area." Smith added some notes to his little black book, without looking up.

"Were you been looking before we met, or just after?" Katlin questioned Smith.

"No, we received a couple calls in regard to this matter. So, I've been here a few times now"

"I hope not from one of our nurses. Martha can get a little carried away."

"Martha says you like to play games?"

"Yes. Do you have any particular game in mind, detective?"

"Just one. How to kill someone without anyone detecting it. Seems to fit in with the deaths we are investigating."

"Yes, it would seem that way, detective. But, like I said before, this is a close team. I would know if something was going on with this crew."

"One more question. You probably have the opportunity to go in and out of any of the rooms on your walks, right?"

"What kinda …" Katlin sputtered in response to what she perceived as Smith's implication.

"Okay, thanks. Here's my card in case you think of anything." Smith handed Katlin a somewhat used-looking card, not giving Katlin a chance to respond to his question.

"Well, you might ask Martha. She seems to have her nose into everything. She's the person you want." Katlin now moved toward her rooms and away from Smith. Flipping into her professional mode, she shot over her shoulder, "If that is all, we need to attend to our patients."

"Thank-you, ma'am. I have had a chat with her and her friends" Smith got the hint and started walking to the doors.

"Wow that seemed odd." Palmer joined Katlin outside of her patient's room. Think he knows something."

"No way. He is out fishing; otherwise, he would have said more."

"Well, it seems odd that he came straight to you."

"Yeah, he may suspect you as well, since everyone knows we take our breaks at the same time, and rumour has it we are sleeping together. Katlin smiled.

"True. Okay, I will watch out for him. I won't say a word, even if he tortures me."

"Oh, fuck you." Katlin laughed.

Stephen did well over night. He managed to rest, and Lisa slept as well after we moved a reclining chair into her husband's room.

"Monday, Stephen will get his shiny new pacemaker. Dr. Bryant said he plans to put in one of the new fancy pacemakers that does everything."

In report today, we learned about a new patient in CCU.

The Game

The bad news was that Dana is a repeat customer. Dana has a severe case of hypercholesterolemia. It is hereditary, and she has passed it on to her two kids. Both are on a statin to keep the levels low. Dana's case is so bad that she needed a heart transplant about six months ago. She is back with us because the arteries of the new heart are closing, and she will die unless she does not get another heart. Some people can wait a lifetime to receive a heart or any organ for that matter. North America has such a demand for organs, it is not funny. Dana is no different. She must have a new heart within the next week, or she will most likely die.

People have all kinds of beliefs or superstitions regarding donation. We, as medical people, can see the difference a new heart makes. A transplant provides a new lease on life for many. However, many people believe they will not enter heaven without all their organs, or if we harvest their eyes, they'll be unable to see when they arrive in heaven. We are a regional transplant center; so, we see firsthand the new life that is awarded to many people. No one is more deserving than Dana and her family. Her husband, Corporal Jack Myers, is an air force pilot, one of the best. He has served his country in two wars. Amy is sixteen, and Jack Jr. is fourteen. The entire family work with Katlin at the Transplant office. They talk to donors, recipients, and health-care workers to increase the awareness about organ donation.

This night, Dana is intubated and sedated because her heart cannot take much stress. We all have to gown up with gloves and masks, even the family. Nothing can be worse than wanting to feel the touch of your family and latex gloves erect a barricade between you.

Tonight, Dana is all mine. I have no other patients. I was the first one she saw when she opened her eyes on her last visit. Therefore, the family asked if I could be her nurse. It was my privilege to be at her side.

The report from Jody the day nurse was not good. Dana's heart function was poor. Her ejection fraction had gone from 62 percent down to 34 percent. The echocardiogram that we did tonight looked even worse. She might die soon. Dana's family never left, and I never asked them to. If we needed to move, lift, or turn her, the family was there. Amy and Jack Sr. washed and bathed her. My entire shift, I was focused on getting her through one more night. Just until a heart becomes available, that is all I ask and all Jack Sr. prayed for.

It was difficult to give medications. The IV medications that we usually give would tax the heart even more than it already was. Dr. Beneventi ordered a small dose of inotropes, which is medication to increase the contractility of the heart. I spent all night going up one or two drops and then down two or three drops per hour, depending on Dana's oxygen consumption and mean arterial pressure (MAP). As each hour passed, Dana became weaker and required a larger dose of her inotropes.

At 3:15 a.m., Jack's prayer was answered, or so he thought. Dr. Beneventi came flying through the doors. The family raced to her.

"Dr. B., what's the news? What's going on?" Amy rushed to the doctor.

"Good news, bad news, I'm afraid. We have a heart!" The family jumped. "However, the heart is at the UCLA

The Game

Medical Center in California. A Lear jet would never make the deadline to retrieve the heart and

return to the hospital in time to transplant into Dana. It takes two hours to get there, two hours back, plus time to pick the heart up and get it into the OR with Dana."

In true military fashion, Jack jumped and said what kind of time do we have?

"Well we need to be at the UCLA in about an hour to receive the heart, return and transplant by 6:00 a.m. Every minute of every hour counts against a good result for her." Dr.B added up the time frame.

Jack ran out the room straight to the phone. What was he doing? I followed out after him as Dr. B. studied Dana's condition.

I got to Jack, already on a phone with the air force.

"Right, I will need my jet in less than thirty minutes. Have it ready" He hung up. I can get to California within the hour."

"What? What do you mean?" I watched Jack as he talked on the phone.

Dr. B. came out of Dana's room, and Jack Sr. laid out the mission.

"My jet is ready now; I can fly to California and be back with the heart before 6:00 a.m. Have your team meet me at the airstrip to transport the heart back to the hospital."

The rest seemed easy. I called the ambulance to take Jack to his plane. Jack was code three with the ambulance to the air force base, nonstop! Jack landed at the LAAFB, which is also the home of the 61st Air Base Group. The medical team had a small red and white cooler for Jack.

"Good luck, Sir." Dr. Morgan, who's part of the transplant team in LA, wished Jack well.

Jack saluted back to the doctor who handed him the cooler.

At 6:30 a.m., Jack arrived via ambulance with his wife's heart in his hands.

Dr. B. and the team were ready; we had transported Dana to the OR. Dana received her second heart.

The night was over for me. Home time and I needed to go work out at the gym. That was a stressful and emotional night. I needed an outlet.

"Katlin, you want to meet me at the gym?" Palmer walked over to Katlin.

"Yeah, or we can go to my place and talk. You look like you need a friend after that emotional night. Dana will pull through; she is tough Palmer, you'll see."

"Okay, I would sooner have a drink than get all sweaty working out."

"Okay, follow me home, Palmer. We can have a drink and talk."

Katlin's house is amazing. It's a large, ranch-style home on the west bank. It's only about 4500 square feet. The west bank is where all the doctors live. It has enough land for her horses. The back of the house leads out to the horse stable and riding grounds. It's very green and well-groomed. The grounds remind me of a smaller version of the ranch on the TV show Dallas—pool and all.

"Scotch is good, if I recall." Katlin reached for the bottle of Highland Park.

"Yeah, that should do. Where is the family today?"

"Meghan is away at her friend's sleepover. Jason is gone.

The Game

He may be in Bakersfield.

"So, have you spoken to him since you tossed him out?"

"No, I asked him to stay at a hotel that day, which he had no trouble with. But today is about you. We don't need to discuss my problems. You did a great job with the family and Dana today. You looked in shock when Jack said he was flying to California."

"Yeah…ha ha, that was kind of cool. Not many people can say that they had their significant other's heart in their hand."

Katlin sat next to Palmer, wrapped her arms around him, and held him tight and longer than usual.

"Is this weird?" Katlin looked up at Palmer.

"No, it just feels familiar."

"Yeah. Thanks for your help last night and now." Palmer looked at Katlin.

Katlin leaned in and kissed Palmer's cheek, "Yes, this does feel familiar."

"I thought we talked about this. We promised ourselves we would not tangle ourselves up again."

"Yes, but I consider you my best friend, Palmer. We talk, we share, and we understand each other. I know we said we would not act on this, but here we are."

"Yes, we are a team. Well, let's just sit here before we give it a try."

"Okay, Palmer, let's relax."

Both sipped on their drinks, but instead of relaxing, they became aware of an uneasiness between them. As Katlin and Palmer sat side by side, contemplating the discussion, Palmer needed to reassure Katlin, and perhaps himself of their mutual feelings. "I'm here for you, Kat," he stated.

THE DAY SHIFT

The day shift is usually very busy. Doctors, interns, lab administration, almost everyone is coming and going. Patients move in and out quickly, depending on their illness or its severity. Today is no different. Janet is in charge again today and ready to get Gilbert Robinson, a forty-seven-year-old male from Texas.

"Arriving via ambulance, Mr. Robinson is a truck driver who was passing through the four corners area when he started sweating and having pain that radiated down his left arm."

"What did the ECG show, Chris?"

"Looks like his circumflex coronary artery is blocked, and he is headed to the Cath lab before you get him."

In many cases, the doctor will take the patient straight to the Cath lab from the emergency room. Dr. Frank Bennett is no exception. He took Mr. Robinson to the Cath lab to open the artery.

"Mr. Robinson, let me explain what going on. The Circumflex (Cx) coronary artery is a branch of the left main coronary artery after it runs its course between the aorta and the main pulmonary artery. The Cx travels in the left atrio-ventricular groove that separates the left atrium from the left ventricle. The Cx moves away from the LAD and wraps around to the back of the heart. So, we plan to open it up and add a stent to the artery."

"Ah, thanks, Doc. What language is that? Can you simplify that for me?"

The Game

"Sure Mr. Robinson. You drove down the 491, which is the main highway right?"

"Yeah." Robinson wasn't sure where this is going.

"And there are other highways like 160 and 64. If 491 is blocked due to a car pileup, you have to take another route. Well, the one artery that goes to the back side of your heart is blocked. Blood can flow through other arteries, but if we don't get the bigger artery open, we cause more damage. The smaller routes you would take are not big enough to carry other big trucks and traffic for long. So, it is best to open the main highway. We are going to build a bridge in this one artery to allow blood to flow easy."

"Okay, I get it. Well, let's open the road." Robinson smiled at Dr. Bennett.

Dr. Bennett takes a few pictures of the artery and slides the stent into place. The patient is sent up to CCU for an overnight stay.

"Hi, Janet. Here is Mr. Robinson. We stented the circumflex artery and left the arterial line in place."

"Thanks, John. I'll get him hooked up to the monitor. We can watch his blood pressure with the arterial line."

"Hi, Mr. Robinson. I'm Janet, your nurse. You will have to lie flat for a few hours till we take out the line in your leg."

"Okay, when can I get back on the road?"

"Mr. Robinson, you just had a heart attack. You need to rest. Let your heart and body recover."

"But I feel good. I need to get back on the road."

One of the problems with getting a patient into the Cath lab and opening the artery so quickly is patients think they are recovered and can go back to the same life style. It's not like years ago when a patient laid in bed and waited to see if they survived the heart attack. Our modern medicine and treatments do get patients out of the hospital quicker, but they still need to rest and let the heart recover.

Days off are a big deal. They give us time to unwind from the stress of the weekend. It's funny, even though we work nights, we still refer to it as *The Day* as in how was your day?

Nurses deal with stress in many ways. Some sleep, some do the housework, work out, run, drink, or see family. Whatever helps to relieve the stress of the night shifts.

The week always seems to go by quickly. If you work nights, you usually lose a day, just to readjust your internal clock. Then we spend time catching up on bills, groceries, or yard work.

"Palmer where you headed this week?" Franco made conversation.

"I'm doing just a short trip to Texas. Be back home by Tuesday"

"That is so cool. What is this week's lecture?"

"Oh, the usual. Time to treatment, Women and MIs, and a little on pacemakers"

"What?" Franco stood a little too close to Palmer.

"Yeah, the company I am doing this for will provide almost any type of training, as long as it is cardiac-related."

"So, you don't have to push the clot-busting drug at every lecture?"

"No, I don't even have to mention it. But people ask about it all the time—how to use it, when, why, that sort of stuff."

I got this gig a few years ago while the hospital had a setup at a convention that hosted a bunch of cardiac doctors.

The Game

Mike Solomon, the representative for a pharmaceutical company that sold a clot-busting drug, asked if we used this clot-busting drug, or thrombolytic, in the air during our transports of cardiac patients. I told him yes, we did. I explained that when I and several of the other CCU nurses were off duty, we were on call for the air ambulance service the hospital had. I laid out how we can relay ECGs to our medical adviser in the ER and receive his instruction to use the thrombolytic or other medications as indicated. After this explanation, Mike Winters asked me do small talks for his company. I accepted and now do lectures in many large and small towns. The lectures included talking about myocardial infarctions, time to treatment, women and MIs, and other relevant topics.

"Don't you get nervous?" Barry stepped into the conversation.

"My first lecture was in front of more than two hundred people at the Texas Heart Institute in Houston. I was so nervous. What can I tell the people that practically invented the artificial heart? I was so nervous that I thought I was going to fall over. I was not sure how to start. Should I tell a joke, or just start explaining the slides. So, I said to the audience, 'I never know how to start a lecture. I have heard too many bad jokes when I was sitting where you are. So, I will not put you through that.' People laughed, and I was able to do the class. One session that I did I asked what people did or where everyone worked. You guys know, you have been to lectures. So, I asked, 'how many people work in CCU?' No one put their hand up. 'How many work in ICU?' No hands. 'How many work in the ER?' Again, no hands.

I was stumped." How many work in Labor and Delivery," thinking I would be funny. Everyone put their hand up."

"What!" Franco half laughed.

"They were all there to get credits for their licence. So, it was one of my best talks on women and heart attacks."

I worked Tuesday through Thursday with them, and changed my schedule to Friday through Sunday in CCU.

"Hey, where are we playing this week?" Barry jumped in after Franco was done.

"It's your pick, buddy. Where do you feel like playing?"

"How 'bout Rustin lake again?" I like the wide-open greens there. Helps for my slice." Barry laughed a little too hard.

We like golfing on Mondays after the night shift was over. Barry, Thomas, and I are always too jacked to go to bed and try to sleep. So, the three of us play golf as often as our schedules allow.

"Barry, I'll be back on Monday late, so we can play Tuesday afternoon."

"Okay, Tuesday it is." Barry was already smiling.

Travel has been getting boring. You get on the plane, get off the plane. Then I rent a car and go to the hotel. In the morning, I drive to the hospital to do the lecture. Once the lecture is over, I am back on the plane and home. It may be time to hang up the lecture circuit.

"Hi guys, thanks for changing our tee time. I needed the extra few hours to sleep."

"Okay, let's get some beer and hit the links!" Thomas was ready to get after it today.

"Okay, a dollar a hole again? Barry felt lucky today.

The Game

"Sure, I can take your money, Barry." Palmer laughed as he warmed up his swing.

Thomas hit the ball the farthest of the three. He is usually the guy to beat, but his short game needs work and that's usually where Palmer and Barry can catch Thomas.

"Hey, Palmer. I heard you had a quiet night with that transplant." Thomas stepped in to hit his usual 250-foot strip down the middle.

"Yeah, it was tough, I kinda got to know the patient and the family well. I hope she is there when I return. She is too young to die, and her kids are way too young to lose a mom."

"I also hear Katlin is taking care of you."

Palmer smiled, "No, we are just friends."

"Yeah, you said that last time and look what happened. You said you would not get involved."

"Wait, what?" Barry stepped back after his sliced golf swing.

"You and Katlin! When was this, where was I?"

"Palmer keeps it quiet because Katlin is married, if you call that a marriage. Is that asshole out of the house yet, Palmer?"

"Sounds like it, Tom. She has asked him to stay somewhere else."

"So, makes room for you?" Thomas smiled as the trio looked for Barry's ball, which had landed in the rough.

"No, we said we would not start anything. I truly like her and do not want to do anything to hurt our friendship. I was over at her house, and we had a couple drinks and talked."

"Found it!" Barry stood over his ball.

"Please do not say anything to anyone, guys. Promise?"

"Yeah, of course Palmer. What is said on the course, stays on the course, right, Barry?"

"Yes, for sure. This is where we can talk and say anything."

"Thanks, Barry. By the way, you suck at golf."

Both Thomas and I laughed as Barry topped his shot, which went only fifty feet. The rest of the game went as per usual—Barry in the rough, myself and Thomas matching each other.

"I need a beer already, guys." Barry reached into his bag for a beer. "You guys?" Barry waved a beer at me and Thomas.

"Sure, Barry, toss me one." Palmer held his hands out.

"Yeah, me too, buddy," Thomas jogged out for a pass, like a wide receiver in football.

By the end of the game, Barry owed me and Thomas each five bucks because he lost the holes.

CHAPTER FIVE

Walking through the bowels of the hospital to the morgue has always felt eerie to Smith. He has been this way too many times in his career. It has just never gotten easy. Mostly because at the end of the hallway was never good news. Death. Young, old, the deserving, and the not deserving awaited him at the end of the hall.

"Hey, Doc. What's up, you called me?"

"Well, howdy, Mr. Detective. Thanks for coming down so quickly. Brooks welcomed the detective into the morgue, his home away from home, and waved the detective in, still with a sandwich in his hand. I got that report back. You were right, something just didn't add up."

The autopsy room is like most. It has stainless steel tables, each with a water hose to clean the bodies off. There are two desks which look like they came from a school class room. Old marked up pine wood with three draws on the left side. Both with a computer and screen on each of them. The medical examiner can dictate from one of the tables and edit the dictation at the desk. Along the one wall are several steel doors. Each door is about four by four feet square. Each door is a stainless-steel slab where the bodies are stored until the mortuary picks up the patient to get them ready for the funeral.

Brooks set his sandwich down on one of the tables before opening the four by four door marked #112. "This lady died of a heart attack, at least that's what it looked like. But I re-examined the body and found a powder around her nose. Very subtle. I sent it off to tox and will get it back soon. But looks like someone made her inhale or gave her something to inhale, which triggered a heart attack. Did you get anywhere with the staff?" Brooks got back to his sandwich.

"Yeah, I have a couple people in mind. Seems we have people wandering the halls at any given time of the day and night."

"Well, that's common in all hospitals. Even during the day people need to get away for a few minutes. You think it's one of our staff?" Brooks closed the fridge door while holding his sandwich in his mouth."

"I agree with what you said before. You said it must be a health-care professional. They have access."

"But what's the motive?" Brooks washed his hands after his lunch.

"Well, I think if we figure the motive out, we will find our killer."

"Okay, my friend, that is your department. How 'bout we meet up for a drink after work?" Brooks turned to Smith as he dried his hands.

"Okay, that's a plan. Thanks, Doc. Gotta run."

"Okay, Smith. I'll keep you posted, and I will buzz you later."

"Hey, by the way, how did Jordan do the other day?"

The Game

"His usual. Struck out a bunch and won the game. He was asked to try out for the traveling team."

"Good for him. You have quite the ball player on your hands."

"Yep, I can retire when he makes the big league." Smith smiled at his own comment.

"Hi, Whitney. How are you?"

"Katlin, what are you doing here during the day?"

"I am here to look at my friend's chart again. I am leaving my purse and things up here on the unit and am heading down to medical records. One of the docs will let me in to view the chart."

"Okay, let me know if you need anything."

"Thanks, Whitney. I'm good for now. See you later."

Whitney is the day charge nurse in CCU this day. She is about 5 foot 7 inches and about 120 pounds. She's a feisty young nurse who works hard and keeps the peace on the unit.

Katlin is in medical records reviewing Mary's chart, making notes, and thinking out loud.

"How do you get a lab result changed?"

"How would the Protamine order get changed so quickly?"

"Why was her allergy not noticed?"

"I need to talk to the laboratory department, then talk to Carly again." Katlin wrote her last few notes before she headed out.

This was a quiet week for me. I only had a short trip and returned home for the rest of my days off. One round of golf and that was it for the week. Hanging out around the house is something that I enjoy. Sitting on the deck listening to

Eleanora Fagan, better known as Billie Holiday is wonderful. Her vocal style, strongly inspired by jazz instrumentalists, is what I like the most.

You can't beat relaxing with a CAO flathead 660 cigar and Caol Ila eighteen-year-old scotch, which comes from Islay whiskies. Listening to vinyl and sipping on scotch is the best.

This is the time to reflect on the past few weeks, thinking of Katlin, work, and the fun I had playing golf. I have tried to played trumpet on and off but could never quite play jazz, just simple, fun tunes. But nonetheless, this was still relaxing. I have a large collection of records, vinyl is the only way to listen to the greats. I never knew what mood I would be in, so having a lot of artists to choose from made things easier.

It was a good day for Lisa. Stephen had his pacemaker implanted and is recovering nicely on the step-down unit. Stephen will get his last dose of prophylactic antibiotics, then probably go home the next day.

CHAPTER SIX

Whenever we started back to work, whether it be Thursday for some or Friday for others, we always got the scoop on the week. This week was all about Dana.

Dana was hanging in there. She was in isolation, but recovering. The family was off the wall. They were so happy to have this time together, it did not matter to them that they all had to gown and glove every time they went into the room.

Guess who has to take care of Dana this weekend? She would be my only patient as any transplant is one-to-one, meaning one nurse for only the one patient. But normally, all the nurses were on the lookout for Dana. Everyone was ready to pitch in to help her and me with whatever was needed. Dana was stable for now, so the routine was the same. Isolation meant that staff who went into the room needed to don a gown, gloves, and mask, any time they needed to do vital signs, assessment, and change dressings. Then they had to take the gown, gloves, and mask off and chart. The big event was packing the massive chest wound that had been open since her last surgery. During that procedure, I exclaimed, "Wow! You can see the lungs expand

and contract and the heart pump the vital blood to and fro." Perhaps this wasn't the most professional outburst, but it was truly awesome.

"Yes, I am getting used to seeing my organs exposed while the nurses do the dressings." Dana responded.

"It's no problem packing the wound, Dana, just time-consuming." I worked on the dressing. It took about an hour to complete. By then, Dana was tired and ready for sleep. I made sure that Dana was comfortable and left her in peace.

Letting the door close quietly behind me, I said more to myself that anyone, "Okay, I need a large coffee now, before I chart and go back in"

Moving toward the coffee machine, I was relieved to see some of the team around the big table. I addressed them collectively, "Dana's wound is not closing; the tissue is too brittle to close with sutures. So, we must let it heal from the inside out. Problem is, the wound is not healing.

We pack it with sterile gauze every four hours. I fear we may have to debride the wound or increase the frequency of changing the dressing to keep it dry.

MIDNIGHT

All is well. No one has died; there have been no codes and no admits. This has been a good night. So, we need to do one round of vital signs on the unit, and we'll have a chance to relax and catch up on the past few days' activity.

"Palmer, we may have a patient coming in who will need your attention."

"Kurt, can you take over for Palmer?"

"Yeah, sure, Ms. Katlin. I can do that." Kurt tried to do the happy to- oblige thing.

"Hey, want to know what I did this weekend?" asked Bev, as if we did not know what was coming. Every week is the same with Bev, so it was unlikely that this story would be a surprise. Bev has no buffer when it comes to talking about sex. She lives, breaths, and dreams sex. Everything reminds her of sex. Inserting an IV into an arm gets her hot.

"Okay, wait. See I went out for a drink and ran in to this guy…Oh, my god! He was so cute!! Six foot, three, eyes were blue, and a chest that was like Hercules. Well, a couple of drinks, and he was coming home with me. I screamed all night long, cause… well you know, he was long all night!" Bev laughed at her own little pun. "When I woke up in the morning and saw him in daylight, and well… he had to be twenty at best. I did everything to that twenty-one or twenty-two-year old." Bev is thirty-five at best. I have another date with, ahhhh! With him."

"Hmm. What was his name?" Katlin smirked at Bev.

"It'll come to me, and if it doesn't, no matter."

"Okay. Thanks for that update Bev," Katlin exclaimed.

Bev also enjoyed travel. She often took short trips to Vegas or Las Angeles. She said traveling helped to clear her head and get her ready to get back to work. Bev is a good nurse, she is quiet about her life with the exception of her sex escapades. I was never sure where she went to school, or if she had lived here all her life.

Bev enjoys going on walks to visit the other floors. She talks about anything and everything. She would make a great used-car salesperson. She loves to talk to whomever she meets. She will be your best friend, unless you piss her off.

"So, Bev, how's the motorcycle coming along?" Katlin changed the topic of conversation.

Bev has a 1953 Indian Chief motorcycle, one from the last year of production. She maintains that this powerful classic, built by the Indian Motorcycle Company, made for a comfortable ride and great conversation starter. At least that is what we learned when asked Bev about her ride.

"I love hitting the road, I meet so many great people."

"Hey, we had a great week as well," Kurt chimed in. "Silvia, the dog, and me."

"So, Silvia and I went into the mountains and spent hours exploring around the woods. Eventually, we found this small cabin that seemed to be abandoned. We went in and checked things out. Inside the shack, we saw old jugs, like moonshine would come in. So, Silvia said to me, 'Wouldn't it be funny to see a still out back?' We went out and looked all over the woods, but did not see anything but a couple of busted barrels. Nevertheless, it is a cool place to hang out. So, we plan to go back next week and explore some more."

The Game

"Oh, man! That's lame. That is all you hippies do is explore and get close to nature." Franco jumped in. "I like to explore, but not the same nature you do. He laughed out loud. "If you know what I mean?"

"Yes, Franco, we get it. You and Ang like to do the wild thing everywhere." Katlin jumped in before the stories got XXX-rated.

Angelika Auchen or Ang as everyone calls her is married to Franco. Ang came from South Africa several years ago, fell in love with Franco, and, as they say, that's all they wrote. They enjoy being together and can't seem to get enough sex from each other.

Franco and Ang also enjoyed hiking. Franco just never mentions this. He always talks about what they do in bed. Both like to ski. They could go high into the mountains, ski for the morning, and come down during the afternoon to explore.

"Well, this week, we went skiing. Ang and I spent the morning on the slopes. I am getting good at the black diamond slope. That's where the fun is. We were skiing down a blue run and crossing over from one run to another. We were having so much fun, we lost our direction and came flying out of the trees and landed on a black run. Ang did a face plant, and it looked like a yard sale with her skies landing beside her and her poles in another area. She looked so funny with snow in her face. Good thing she was okay."

"That doesn't sound funny." Bev scolded Franco.

Kurt looks nothing like a nurse. Kurt ran a construction business for several years until the jobs dried up, and Kurt needed to make money. Kurt looks like he should be in the mountains, hunting and fishing. He is six feet, four inches tall, with dark brown, wavy hair, and a beard. He and Silvia actually do live up in the mountains, in a very nice, quiet place. But it has all the amenities of town living.

Silvia is a small fit person and full of energy. She completed her Bachelor of Science in Nursing (BSN) ages ago and has been in ICU for years. Silvia is very nice; she's an attractive, down-to-earth person. She isn't like some critical care nurses who are uptight or know-it-alls—just a great nurse and person. I'm not sure how Kurt and Silvia met. They have never told us. They were married some while ago, but they have no paper to show of the marriage. Kurt said that they had friends over and told each other they loved one another, and then they had a party! I think they met while they were in nursing school and just hit it off. But Kurt won't confirm this. Silvia responds by saying, "I don't know, what did Kurt say?"

"Yeah, well, what did you do, Ms. Katlin?" asked Franco respectfully. Katlin is the elite of our team. When she talks, everyone listens. Katlin is elegant and has a past that has never been made clear, but we always imagine what she was like. I think she liked to party and be out with friends. I know she loved concerts because she will sometimes say 'I remember this concert we went to' and then go on with her story. She was, or perhaps still is, a free spirit.

Katlin has doctors asking her out all the time. She reminds them that she is married, but tells them she will let them know if things change. She did have her eye on one doctor. They were forever talking in the back room or off to the side. She didn't really talk much about that, but you knew she was looking.

"Well, I will have you know that I spent an amazing weekend with my daughter—relaxing, horseback riding, eating healthy lunches, and having long talks..."

"Yeah, yeah!" Franco jumped in. "We all know it was amazing." With his tongue in his cheek, he continued, "It was a hallmark moment."

"Bite me, Franco! Some people actually have a normal life and enjoy the simple pleasures of their family. I enjoy spending time with my daughter. She is old enough now that she is like a sister or another good friend."

Katlin spends time reading books and listening to old rock. She is a big fan of Prince, ACDC, and The Stones. If she is not reading a book, she is cooking. Katlin is a good chef and can cook almost anything.

"We had a good game of golf." Barry got in on the conversation. "I spent the rest of the week making my beer. You guys need to come over and try it."

"Well, that sounds like a plan." Palmer stood and sipped his coffee.

"What did you do, anything fun?" Bev looked up at Palmer.

"No, I just traveled for one lecture and back, then stayed at home to rest up for this weekend."

"Well, that's no fun! Call me next time." Bev winked at Palmer.

"Bev, I wouldn't know what to do." Palmer smiled as Bev flung her hair back over her left shoulder.

"Hey, guys. Whatz up!?" Victor crashed our conversation. "Did you hear about that patient that bit the big one last week? The pathologist thinks something funny happened to the patient, and Glover and the detective are going to question the staff down on second floor."

"Oh!" Katlin sounded surprised. "What did they find? Was that Detective Smith involved?"

"Who is Smith?" Victor questioned, but he didn't seem really interested. "Not sure, but looks like someone gave too much of a drug, or maybe withheld a drug, not sure but they are pulling the staff in." Victor didn't bother to wait for Katlin to respond.

"That seems odd. Do they do that on a regular basis?" Bev asked.

"No, that's what is weird" Victor continued. "This is a first, so it must be serious."

"Well, they came and talked to us already," Barry added.

"Oh, wow! That is nuts, man. What did they ask?"

"Nothing, just if we saw anyone suspicious."

"Doesn't matter. Well, gotta run, people." Victor looked at Barry as he headed to the door.

Well that's rude." Barry looked around to see who was still listening.

The phone rings, and it is the ER. Dr. Steiner has a young twenty-one-year old female there who has an internal, implanted defibrillator that keeps going off.

"She has short runs of ventricular tachycardia. She is starting to decompensate and needs a bed."

"Okay, bring her up." Katlin took a few notes from Dr. Steiner.

"What's up, Katlin!"

The Game

"You are getting the young girl in ventricular tachycardia and a malfunctioning AICD that I mentioned earlier. Dr. Steiner is bringing her up."

"Okay, I'll get the bed ready, Katlin."

"Thanks, Palmer."

Getting the bed ready means that we get the entire room set up for any potential risk. In this case, I made room for the ventilator, prepared large 10cc syringes with Versed, and prepped another syringe

with morphine. That way, I could administer medications quickly, without having to mess with the small vials if an emergency situation arose.

Dr. Steiner came through the door and inquired, "Who is getting her?"

"I am, sir."

Dr. Steiner is an older cardiologist with the big group. He is old school and can detect heart disease and problems from a block away. Dr. Steiner deserves respect from all of us. I never address a doctor by their first name. I have always felt that showed disrespect. Even if the doctor said, call me by my first name, or if I knew them away from the hospital.

"Okay, this girl will most likely need to be intubated, and we need to get her on the heart transplant list. I did an echo, the ejection fraction has gone from normal to about 30 percent in just a few hours. Probably due to the continuous cardio shocks her device is giving her. We have tried all meds, nothing works. Her chemistry is fine, so I'm not sure what we can do for her. The higher we go with inotropes, the worse it is. We can't tax her heart much more, or she will die." Dr. Steiner stood over the team while he filled Palmer in.

Sara arrived upstairs, and we needed to intubate, sedate her, and try to figure this out. After we got her settled and our lines in place, we tried to optimize her medications, oxygen, and the other usual options. Nothing worked.

"You know she came into the office and the defibrillator was not as active as it is now. The internal cardiac defibrillator reads the rapid rhythm Sara's heart is in and delivers an electrical current to hopefully reset the heart rhythm. The problem is the rhythm continues to return, thus she is being shocked, or defibrillated much too often. This is why I called for an ambulance to transport her from the office to the hospital."

"What do you think it is? Is the AICD reading something else?"

"No, Palmer, I had the interrogation machine on and she is really having runs of VT."

"Barry, can you have the echo technician come up? We need to see the ejection fraction again."

"Sure, Dr. Steiner. Will do." Barry was already punching in the number.

Dr. Wenich arrived to help with the intubation of Sara to help her breath. "Hi, Dr. Steiner. She's intubated and quiet now. I just finished intubating her"

"Thanks, Adam. That will buy her some time while we figure this out."

"Anything I can do, Dr. Steiner?"

"No. I called Dr. Muñoz from infectious disease to see if he has any ideas."

The Game

"Oh, good. Donald is a good ID person. Well, I am out of here. Let me know if I can help." Dr. Adam Wenich walked out the door.

"Hi, Loretta. The patient is in here with Palmer." Barry ushered in the echo technician.

"Hey, Loretta. Go ahead. I can work around you." Palmer organized the IV lines so they wouldn't be in the technician's way.

"Thanks, Palmer. I shouldn't be too long. I did the other echoes downstairs before she got up here."

Dr. Steiner looked over Loretta's shoulder. "Oh my, we need to list her for a transplant. This looks less than the last echo."

"Yeah, her ejection fraction is down to about 23 percent." Loretta did her measurements of the left ventricle. Sara's heart was barely moving. On the echo, it looked like just her valves were moving. Her blood pressure was dropping, and we still had no reason for the ventricular tachycardia or device malfunction.

"If we shut the device off, we would need to shock her every five minutes, so best to leave the device on." Dr. Steiner ran through options.

"Palmer, did you start the dopamine to keep her blood pressure up?"

"I did. But even at this low dose, we are taxing her heart."

"Does anyone have any ideas?" Dr. Steiner was always willing to listen to anyone.

"Well, I might!"

"Well, what is it? Let's hear it, Palmer."

"Well, our transplant team has a new protocol in the works for our donors."

"Palmer, we are not ready to donate organs! Even if we were, her heart is not worth much."

"I know. Hear me out. Using all these inotropes on donors taxes the heart and makes the heart less viable because of the oxygen consumption. So, we give a bolus of the thyroid medication T-4, then hang a T3 drip. The T-4 converts to T-3 in the body, but the bolus helps to raise the levels quickly to get a rapid response. This allows the thyroid meds to increase the chronotropic effect of the heart to increase without taxing the heart like dopamine, dobutamine, or isuprel would."

"Wait, so an increase in chronotropic affect means it will help the heart to pump stronger, right?" Barry tried to follow the logic.

"Yes, Barry. The thyroid levels increase by giving these two thyroid medications, which helps the heart to push blood out to all organs "

"Well, yes, that is the pharmacokinetics of these thyroid medicines. But, has it been tried?" Dr. Steiner looked at Palmer and Katlin.

"Well, we have used it on a couple donors, and it seemed to work." Palmer looked at Dr. Steiner.

"Katlin, is this correct?"

"Yes, Dr. Steiner. We have tried it."

"We'll need to monitor the potassium and glucose levels every fifteen minutes because as these thyroids meds increase some of the blood levels, while other levels will decrease."

The Game

"If you can just sign the orders for me, which are several, we can start."

"Okay, Palmer. It's your game."

I ran to my locker to get protocol and went to work. Within the first four hours, the ejection fraction increased to about 40 percent. By six hours, we were able to extubate Sara. By the time the day staff arrived, Sara was sitting up, talking, and feeling good. The EF increased to near normal. That night, when we arrived back, Sara was able to move around. Dr. Steiner was already on the unit, looking through the chart at the bedside.

"Sara, do you work with animals, or are you around several pets?" Dr. Steiner sat at the end of her bed.

"Yes, I work with several horses every day." Sara replied with a raspy voice from the breathing tube that had been down her throat. "Why, doctor? Why do you ask?"

"Well, one of our infectious disease doctors, Dr. Donald Muñoz, found salmonella in your blood stream. It was this type of infection that caused your heart to beat erratically, and ultimately caused your device to trigger until your heart became so weak, it could hardly pump blood to your other organs. It must have been the feces from the horses. You must have come in contact with the feces, which gave you the salmonella poisoning."

"Oh my, I clean the barn and horse stables every day. I must have toughed the horse poop, or slopped it which could have landed on my face or something like that."

Once Sara was stable, they took her in for a new defibrillator. She was due for a replacement next year, but this incident prompted them to give her a new one.

Word got to the other cardiologists in that group. The group asked Katlin and me to join a weekly meeting to present this case with Dr. Steiner.

"How the hell does a nurse know this shit, and we don't?" Dr. Bennett said with concern and pride that he had nurses who can think.

"Simple, we are nurses." I smiled at the roomful of cardiologists.

I discussed the protocol that we used, which prompted the doctors to make sure this was implemented for our donor program.

"We need the two of you to join our group as nurse specialists." Dr. Bennett looked at his team and got approving nods from the others. If the cardiology group saw nurses who did a great job, they tried to recruit them to work for their team. Katlin and I passed, for now.

CHAPTER SEVEN

"I read an article about a nurse killing patients with insulin. I think I can do that. I can push the insulin through the IV and get out before anything happens. I'm beginning not to feel anything when I do this. Does this make me a bad person? Well it's for the better good."

Like most Fridays, we catch up on the week on the unit. It's funny that a conversation from last week carries over to this week like we were never gone.

"You guys made that shit up, didn't you?" Franco asked in amazement. He was referring to Sara's case from the previous week.

"Well, it worked didn't it?" Katlin smiled. "Some days are just better than others." Not wasting time on details, Katlin changed direction. "Okay, let me know what your patients are up to."

The night was quiet; there was nothing out of the ordinary. This gave us all a chance to take regular breaks and relax a little. First order of business was to make sure all patients were cared for. If someone was in their room working, we jumped in to help out. It was not cool to abandon your colleagues while they are working and you are not. Many times, we would go into a room and help turn a patient or just clean up. Baths were usually done with two or three nurses, depending on how large or sick a patient was.

"Palmer, after the patients are tucked away, do you want to go for a walk?" Katlin asked.

"Sure, let me finish my charting, and I'll be ready." I always made sure charting was up-to-the-minute. You never knew when things would go sideways.

"Hey, guys, we are going on break. Watch our patients, please."

"Okay, you kids have fun." Bev waved as Katlin and I headed to the doors.

"Let's do our usual route, Katlin," I suggested as we walked out the door. "How are things, Katlin? Any news from your husband?"

"Oh, he's still gone. I think we are done. Actually, I know we're done."

"Really?"

"Yeah, I am going to file for a divorce. I have had it. I need to move on with my life. I can't wait for him to grow up. Jason was always like this. Very flighty. He would get an idea and go do it. He sees a pretty girl, and has to go do that." Katlin smiled a little after that.

The Game

We stopped in the stairwell because Katlin looked upset, and we sat on the steps. Clearly this situation was taking a toll on her.

"Let me know if you don't want to talk about it. I don't want to pry."

"No, its fine. I would rather vent to you than to anyone else."

"I guess you need to do what's best for you and Meghan." She put her arms around me, and we just held each other for a while.

"Why can't guys be like you? You're kind, and you listen."

"No, I am not all that. I have my secrets as well. Some that I'll never share."

"Yes, I know some of them." We both smiled; then Katlin kissed me. This kiss was a different kind of kiss than previous ones; it had more to it. We got up and continued on our journey.

"You know, this thing about someone killing patients is scary'" Katlin changed the topic as we walked through the gloomy, poorly lit hallways.

"Yeah, scary because that detective thinks you or I are in on it."

"No, not anymore. Last week, I came into the hospital to look through Mary's chart again. I've talked to Smith a couple times, he even asked Carly to share the chart with him."

"Well, that's good, but what can you learn from the chart?"

"Because I could not see any evidence that she received any medications. That "50" we saw bugged me. I think someone added that number. I can't think of how a lab test would get changed."

"Well, that's easy, Kat. The patient next to her had heparin running. So, you draw her blood and say it's from Mary. The tube is labeled with Mary's name and sent to the lab. The results were high because of the heparin. But instead of giving 5 mg, they give 50mg."

"Yeah, I guess it would be easy to change a label." Katlin tried to understand the process.

"I called Smith and reported the changed medication dose and lab result. He agreed with me, and asked me to keep him posted on what we see or hear. He said he missed the "50" that we found."

"So, who could it be, Palmer?"

"Well, someone who can move throughout the hospital and not be noticed."

"It has to be someone that knows how orders are taken, labs drawn and sent. Give medication via several routes. But the person is following our game. Potassium IV, Protamine IV, those eyes drops." Katlin thought back to all deaths.

"Yeah, the killer is getting better. Didn't they start with the eye drops?" Palmer also reviewed the facts.

"Correct!" Katlin constructed the events like a master sleuth.

"But that's almost everyone." Palmer flipped his hands up to the sky.

"Well, yes, but only night shift. All the deaths have been during the weekend night shifts. So, that narrows it down somewhat."

"Yes, except for Mary. Someone changed her notes to *No known allergies*, changed the dose, and changed the lab tube. That's a lot of work, for what?" Palmer still puzzled.

The Game

"True, but again, someone could have changed that at any time, right?"

"Well, Kat, yes. But it looks like it occurred just before shift change."

"Hey, you're getting good at this detective stuff, Palmer. Not just another pretty face." Katlin smiled as they got to ICSU. The unit was quiet, which meant they were having a good night. No nurses or technicians were running in and out of rooms. The only activity was just at the end of the hall where we noticed Victor coming out of a room.

"Hey, whatz up, you two?" Victor asked somewhat nervously. He might have known what Katlin and Palmer were doing, but he did not ask.

"Just on our way back to the unit. You?" Katlin asked.

"Yeah, just doing treatments." Victor was somewhat out of breath.

"This is an odd time, isn't it? I thought you did treatments every two hours?" Palmer questioned.

"Yeah, well they wanted me to check on a patient." Victor walked back into the room, as Katlin and I followed.

"This lady is diabetic and also has some pulmonary distress. Do me a favour and check in on this lady for me. I have to run upstairs for another treatment." Victor said as he started to walk away. Victor left and we did a quick assessment. Diana walked in just as we finished.

"Hey, guys, what are you doing in my room?"

"Oh, just checking her respirations for Victor." Palmer smiled at Diana.

"Oh, where is he?"

"Not sure, is he not out there? He did say he was headed upstairs."

"No, didn't see him." Diana looked puzzled by this encounter.

"Well, when he comes back, tell him the treatment must have worked. Her breath sounds are clear."

Once we got back to the unit, we had to start our vitals, assessments, and turning our patients. Barry was busy charting and checking charts for missed orders, which was also part of our routine. Sometimes an order is missed or not written, so we need to verify the orders.

Bev and Franco came out of a patient's room.

"Thanks, Franco, that guy is heavy."

"No problem, ma'am."

CODE BLUE, ICSU….. CODE BLUE ICSU. The overhead announcement went.

"Wow, we were just there." Katlin looked at Kurt.

Kurt grabbed the defibrillator and was off.

"My turn, Silvia is running codes for ICU, so I want to go."

Kurt made it to ICSU, and started in on the patient. Diana the floor nurse was already in working on the patient. Usually the floor nurse lowers the bed and gets everything ready for the code team. Diana had already done that and was doing chest compressions. The emergency doc arrived.

"What's going on?" Dr. Connors from the ER assessed the situation.

"Well, this subject was doing well. I was just in here with Katlin and Palmer. Next thing I know, the heart monitor alarmed. I found her unresponsive."

The Game

"Okay, I have a line in, let's give her epi, right, Doc?"

"Yes, Silvia. Diana, are you okay doing compressions? Let us know if you need to change."

"Right, will do."

"Kurt, what does the rhythm look like?"

"Asystole or fine VF."

"Okay, I will intubate the patient; then, let's get some gases and labs, stat." The patient was intubated and ACLS progressed as usual.

"Tara, go ahead and bag her with one hundred percent oxygen."

"Will do, doc." Tara slowly placed the ambu bag on the ET tube.

"Charging to 200.......CLEAR." Thump! the body jerked up and back into the bed. Nothing on the monitor. "Charging to 250......CLEAR." The body jerked again. "Charging to 300....CLEAR." Thump! "Nothing on the monitor." Kurt reviewed the paper rhythm strip after his defibrillation attempts.

"Try Epinephrine again, then atropine." Dr. Connors was running out of options.

They drew blood gases and potassium levels to analysis the effect that they might have accomplished.

"Yeah, these gases are acidotic. Let's try a dose of glucose." Dr. Connor looked at the patient.

"This is so unexpected; the patient was doing well." Diana stated. Matter of fact, Palmer and Katlin were just here and said all was okay. This lady was a diabetic patient and due to go home in a day or so."

"Okay, let's call it, unless anyone has a final idea? No pulse. Go ahead and stop."

Kurt returned to the unit. "She died."

"What was the problem?" Katlin walked toward Kurt.

"Not sure, she had no pulse when we hooked her up. Perhaps, it was just her time. Diana said you guys were there just a few minutes before."

"Oh!" Katlin sounded surprised. "That lady was doing well. Victor came out of the room as we were walking by and said he had given her a breathing treatment. He asked us to check on her because he needed to get something. So, we left her in good shape. How weird."

"Yeah, that is Katlin. Do you think this was on purpose?" Kurt put the defibrillator back on the table.

"Yes, it could be, it does seem sudden."

"Okay what did you guys do?" Franco came into the conversation.

"Victor seemed to want to get out of there in a hurry… You don't think?" Katlin looked at Palmer.

"No, why would he want to kill someone?"

"Well he was a little out of breath, but it might be his asthma acting up." Katlin rationalized his presence.

"I might let Smith know this. I'm sure he will find this interesting. I will call him."

"I am going to check my patients, Kat."

"Okay, good plan. Has everyone looked in on their patients?"

"Yes, mom, we have." Bev laughed at the tone of Katlin's voice.

"Hey, let's play our game, guys!" Barry sat at the table.

The Game

"Barry, I'm not into it tonight. This was a little hard." Kurt walked away from the group.

"Yeah, same." Bev went for coffee.

The team broke off, each member choosing to do their own thing. It seemed quiet for the remainder of the shift. I think this shook us up. Perhaps too close to what sounds like another murder.

The rest of the weekend was uneventful. We all left for our days off.

CHAPTER EIGHT

ANOTHER NIGHT SHIFT

This night started with a bang. One of our administrators arrived with a massive heart attack and on an intra-aortic balloon pump (IABP). The patient was in acute heart failure. Because his heart was unable to pump sufficient blood to meet the metabolic needs of the body, we gave him medication to help relax the venous vascular smooth muscles, but the meds weren't enough, and we had to use the IABP. The IABP counter pulsation elevated the diastolic aortic pressure and augmented the coronary artery blood flow while reducing the heart's workload. We used this to try to maintain viable perfusion pressure due to the severity of Mr. Chester Davis's heart damage. We hoped this would buy time for a heart transplant.

"I will take, Chester. I know him and the family." Katlin announced to the team.

Katlin wanted this patient because she knew Mr. Davis. She felt he was a good person and a real advocate for CCU and the heart transplant program. She knew that Mr. Davis had pushed for nurses to manage full patient care and was, in part, the reason we had received extensive training on the IABP, ECMO, and other procedures. Katlin worked hard with Mr. Davis over the weekend. Her plan was to keep him alive until we could find a transplant. It seemed ironic that he needed a heart, and none was available when he needed one.

We all were there for him and Katlin. She would just ask, and the team was there to assist in making him comfortable at all times. The family would come in to visit, but they would just stare at him and leave. They were numb and didn't know what to ask or say, other than thanks.

The night and the remaining part of the weekend were very tense. Doctors and other administrators came and went, checking on him. None of them had any good news to report, critically stable were the best words they could use. The problem was, we were maxed out of medications, and the IABP

was only marginally effective. At least, Davis was sedated and did not know what was going on. Being awake, intubated, and unable to move or turn would have been torture. Keeping him sedated helped.

"Katlin, how is Mr. Davis?" Mr. Glover came in for an update.

"Mr. Davis is slowly deteriorating, Richard. Each day he seems to be worse. I can't seem to keep him stable. Every time we get the drips and IAPB set, he decompensates and I start all over."

From my perspective, what was really bad was the toll it took on Katlin. The harder she worked on titrating drips and fine-tuning the IABP, the worse it seemed to be. The doctors

The Game

tried everything to improve hemodynamics, but to no avail. You could tell Katlin was struggling with Mr. Davis's condition; you just had to look at her face and you knew.

"I'm lost," Katlin admitted after a week of caring for Mr. Davis. "What am I missing?"

"Well, the fact that all arteries are blocked, and his ejection fraction is slightly higher than a ticking second hand of a clock." Palmer tried to lighten the mood. It didn't work. "Katlin, you have done everything, but in your own words, people don't cooperate, they die." My philosophy is when it's time, it's time. "You can be walking across the street, or your plane is hijacked and gets blown up."

"I know. I get it, but there must be something."

"We need a heart transplant, Kat, but that may take a miracle."

"Can we go to Logan's at the end of our shift?" Katlin looked defeated.

"You want me to ask the team?"

"No, just you and me. I just need a drink and to talk."

"Sure, no problem."

Victor would come in to check vent settings and make adjustments. He was there more often than not, because he too knew Mr. Davis and his contributions to the hospital.

"Hola, guys and gals. Whatz up?"

"I think we need to make some vent settings, Victor. His oxygen consumption is slowly rising." Katlin reported to Victor.

"Okay, let me do my thing, and see what we can do."

"Thanks, Victor."

"Hey, anything for you, Ma'am. Hey, it's a full moon out there tonight. You know what that means." Victor laughed.

"Stop that crap, already." Katlin showed her frazzled nerves. "I hate when people say that weird stuff happens every full moon. Shit happens every day, but no one notices it. Come full moon, and it's all blamed on the moon."

I'm not sure why, but all kinds of weird stuff does happen with a full moon. People do weird stuff and weird things happen. In the hospital, we just deal with whatever happens.

Now, I'm not a big believer in ghosts or weird phenomena, but one night we were working on my patient. He was dying; thus, we were coding him. We had all worked hard to save him, but when it's time, it's time. Mr. Erickson died. I cleaned him up and cleaned the room prior to the family coming in. They said their good byes, and then I said my good bye. No matter what people say, some people just grow on you. We had a call from the ER. A patient was having a heart attack and needed a bed. I said "Give us ten minutes to deliver Mr. Erickson to the morgue, and we will take the new patient." Fifteen minutes later, the new patient arrives at the same room that Mr. Erickson had just died in. Mr. Harris was sick, and we were trying to save his life. Mr. Harris was not doing well. He was staring off into the corner, which is never a good thing. I finally asked Mr. Harris what he was looking at off in the corner.

"Who is that man in the corner?" he asked.

I looked around, but no one was there. "I don't see any one, sir."

The Game

Mr. Harris repeated himself, then continued to describe a man who looked identical to Mr. Erickson. Neither man had ever seen the other prior to that moment. Mr. Harris died.

CODE BLUE, EMERGENCY ROOM, CODE BLUE EMERGENCY ROOM.

"Well, that never happens." Victor smirked.

As I arrived in the ER, it was chaos. Police officers were all over the department. Doors were locked; everyone and everything was locked down.

"What the hell is going on," I questioned.

"A gangbanger was dropped off with a GSW to the back. It's lodged in his spine," Dr. Liang replied. "We had him stable until his friends, or rather the gang that shot him came right into the ER and fired one shot that hit him in the aorta. That finished him. We are trying to keep him alive, but he's not got much luck. We sent blood work and gases to the lab, so we will have him cross-matched soon, then we can give him more blood. We'll have to see what happens." Dr. Liang sounded like he was dictating his report already.

"I have to take a patient back to the OR, but I am around if you need me. Dr. Liang looked at the ER doc and me. "You guys have everything well in hand. We are well trained in trauma and ACLS.

Sally the head nurse in ER was checking the patient's personal stuff to see if he had a name and address. This is a routine procedure, as the hospital needs to notify family or next of kin.

"Oh my god!!! He is an organ donor. What kind of banger is a donor?" Sally screamed down the hall to whomever was listening. "Let's start the donor protocol. He is close to death, and we can ship his organs out. He is already on a ventilator and his hemodynamics are dropping fast. The doctors can't do anything." This kid was dying.

It's way too common for these gangbangers to get dropped off at our doors. I guess the gangs figure they can leave the mess for the ER team to clean up. After this little incident, the hospital added bulletproof glass and doors to protect the staff. This gang only wanted this kid; they never looked at or fired a shot at anyone else. FULL MOON.

CODE BLUE CCU, CODE BLUE CCU... the voice from the PA system seemed to startle everyone.

"Well, that's my song they're playing. Gotta run."

I ran up the stairs to CCU. As I got about half way, it struck me as to whom the code was for.... I ran faster.

"Katlin, what's up?" Like I didn't know. Mr. Davis had had enough, he is circling the drain, so to speak.

"I can't keep him going till morning." Katlin announced in a soft voice.

Kurt was doing CPR while Victor was bagging Mr. Davis with 100 percent oxygen, Silvia was giving huge volumes of inotropes to keep the heart ticking, but we were losing Chester. The monitor was showing a flat line. He was gone—no rhythm, no heart sounds.

Dr. Sandoval announced, "Let's call this. Time 23:55."

The door burst open, "Let's go. We have a heart. The kid downstairs is a match to Chester!"

Just as this was announced, Katlin broke down into tears. "He's... he's dead, sir."

The Game

"What?" Dr. Liang looked shocked. "But we have it."

"He died ten minutes ago. Sorry, I tried." Katlin walked out of the room.

"You know that drink we're having? Well, it's going to be a few."

Katlin went out to write her report in the chart while the rest of us cleaned up Mr. Davis and the room.

Logan's Roadhouse has the usual suspects in at this hour—Nurses, hospital staff, and the odd drunk. Logan's is one of the few bars that would be open at this hour. They open at 7:00 a.m. and close at 1:00 a.m. Logan's is pretty typical – nondescript with the usual Bud, Coors, and Coke signs and plenty of racing car pictures on the walls. It's dark, which probably covers up most of the dirt. But the drinks are cheap, the pours full, and the glasses the only clean items in the house. The bar has seven large-screen TVs, each with a different sports channels tuned in, which is nice. The bar holds about twenty patrons with small booths around the perimeter and the usual tall tables and stools closer to the bar. The back area is a restaurant and family area, used only during the supper hour. In the corner of the bar are two large tables that seat ten or more. When we go in, that's where we sit, no matter if there are two or ten of us. Country music is on all the time. Logan's has small pails of peanuts in the shell on every table and, more often than not, the shells land on the floor. The dust from the peanuts is everywhere. They make the best smoked-meat sandwiches around, and the beer on tap is ice cold. Whiskey is always poured very generously. This is our hangout. No one bugs you, so you can drink in peace. People come in, in groups or by themselves, just to escape the day, the night, or anything else they want to get away from for a few hours.

Katlin and I walked into the bar, and Jerry started to pour rye and coke, large. He set it in front of Katlin, who responded, "Thanks, Jer."

"How you doing, Kat?" Jerry asked with a half-smile. As for me, my mouth was wide-open, and I was stunned.

"You come here often?"

"No." Katlin said with a sinister smile. "No, but Jer knows when I do come in, something is up. He and I go way back. Jer knows what I like. It's a story for another time."

"Okay, that's cool, I get it."

Jerry is a tall man and is about sixty-years old. Katlin is nowhere close to that age. Jer looks like an old cowboy who has seen a lot in his lifetime. Jer is quiet, but he looks intimidating. For an older guy, he is still very strong and muscular. He sports a cowboy hat, boots, and denim overalls. A few tattoos are visible on his arms. A couple or the tats look like they might have been done somewhere other than a downtown shop.

We had a couple more drinks and found a few things to laugh at, which helped both of us relax.

"I hate nights like this. No matter what, you can't do a thing. What's the point, Palmer?"

Jer brought both us another drink. He could see this was not a pleasant talk.

"On the house, Kat. Not sure what's up, but don't piss her off, dude!"

The Game

"Thanks, Jerry. No worries, he is my shoulder tonight… this morning, whatever the fuck time it is. Palmer, meet Jerry; Jerry, Palmer."

"Hey, man. How you doin'?"

"Good, Jerry. Just a bad night at the big house."

"Okay, Kat, Palmer. No worries. Chill here for a while." Jer headed back to the bar.

Katlin smiled now. "He's my bodyguard and a good listener."

"I get it; it's all good."

Katlin picked up from where we left off. "I've helped them live, die, laugh, and cry; but this one hurt."

"Chester was a long-time friend. His daughter and Meg rode horses together for years. Our family is close to them. His wife, Jennifer, is a doll. We skied together many times up in Telluride and Breckenridge."

"I hear you. You were close to him before all this happened. Same with the family. We all know you did everything you could. You went above and beyond." Palmer rambled and put his arm around Katlin to comfort her. "What is up with the police and that detective questioning the nurses on second floor?" Palmer attempted to change the topic.

"Not sure, Palmer. This is odd. They seem to suspect someone from the hospital."

"Do you think they still suspect us?"

"Well, no. Not since I spoke to Smith. But who killed my friend Mary?"

"Yeah, I looked at her chart, and there is no reason for her death. So, I looked the chart over, and I called the detective already."

"Yes, that's right. You mentioned that already. Sorry, Kat."

"Yeah, but it does look funny that we were the last to see that lady on ICSU, the diabetic."

"I agree. But Smith wants me to look around a little. I had called him about that lady, he wants me to watch for anything funny. You ready?" Katlin was already standing.

"Sure. Where are we going?"

"My place. We can have another drink and kick our shoes off."

"Well, okay. I'll follow you, Kat. I get lost in the valley."

She laughed, "I like that."

"Thanks, Jerry." Katlin walked to the bar.

"No problem, Kat. Let me know what I can do."

"Thanks, just a tough night— rather a tough week with a patient. See you again, boss!"

"You too, Kat."

It's a bit of a drive to the valley, but it's on my way home. The sun seems full and bright like a new beginning. But, in the distance, the full moon is setting. Weird.

Katlin's land is called Crooked Creek Vineyard and Farm, which is nestled up against the hillside with lush pastures, fruit trees, and grape vines laid out at your feet with McClermo Creek meandering gracefully through the heart of the property.

The home is exquisite with accents of granite, slate, tile, and exposed logs. The house is set up for entertaining. It's only about 4500 thousand square feet, and the land is like a hundred acres or so.

"Here you go, Mr."

Handing me a Scotch, Katlin seems to be more light-hearted than she had been in the bar just a short time ago.

The Game

"Let me show you something," Katlin called as she headed to the back of the house."

"Yeah! What you want to show me? You buy more horses?"

The next sequence caught me off guard.

"Just this. I need to be close to you. I need you now. I know we said this would not happen, but I lied."

The thing about scrubs is, one pull of a string, and you have nothing on. We fell onto her king-size bed with plush white comforter and with the rush of the moment, the excitement mixed with the drinks, we lost all inhibitions. Was the room spinning from the drinks or the warmth of her body against mine? Katlin was fit, that was easy to tell each day at work. She rode horses, hiked, and worked hard around the acreage. But here, now, she was amazing. She moved with the ease of a dancer; I needed to keep up with her. Kissing her neck sparked a reaction, she moaned and turned her head, wanting more. Her nails dug into my back, grabbing her hands and pulling them over her head, I kissed her neck again, making my way down to her breasts. I took my time rediscovering her curves. Like I had done before. Katlin rolled over onto me, looking deep into my eyes. She hesitated for a moment, but then she mounted me. Slowly, Katlin gripped me harder and harder. Katlin now squeezed her legs tight around me, like she did when she's riding a horse. Katlin rocked back and forth while her head stretched back with her eyes closed. I rolled her over, the morning sun flickered around the junipers and in through the window made her skin glow. The curtains flowing from the slight breeze through the open window kept us cool. Katlin wrestled until she was back on top. Both of us moaning in pleasure. Her uncontrollable spasmodic actions caused her to fall off me. We laid side-by-side, breathing heavily and laughing at her fall.

"Oops, sorry. I didn't mean to do that. Are you okay?"

"Yes, Kat, takes more than that to damage anything."

We lost all track of time, and I hated to just jump out of bed, but I did. Katlin understood.

"Do you want me to stay?" But those didn't seem like the right words.

"No, it's okay, Matt. It's fine."

"Matt? You haven't called me that since well, I'm not sure. Palmer smiled at the slip.

"I will see you tonight at work." Katlin held Palmer's hand.

Palmer leaned over and gave Katlin a long slow kiss. "Talk soon, Kat."

THE LAST NIGHT

The shift started as usual. We arrived as we normally do. Barry came in no less than a half hour prior to the start of the shift. Sometimes he arrives an hour before the start, but not tonight. Katlin and I usually arrive close to the same time each shift. We arrive about fifteen to thirty minutes before. Mostly, we like to have a coffee and ease into the night. If it's crazy, at least we can get geared up for that kind of night. Bev and Kurt showed up next. Franco is always five minutes late. If we have extra staff joining us, they always seem to arrive fifteen minutes after report starts. Not that it matters, we give them the easiest patients we have. Mostly so they don't go and kill anyone for one night.

It was different this night. Mr. Davis's room was empty, and the lights were out.

The patient load was not bad—almost like a holiday. I got an elderly gentleman who had large anterior, lateral myocardial infarction. He was lucky. They had placed a couple of stents in and opened up the two blockages. We had the usual mixture of patients tonight—fresh heart attacks, stent placements, and a couple of patients who were just resting on the unit. We often try to keep a patient in case we need to double up for an emergency. Room 5 was eerily empty. No one wanted to admit a patient into Mr. Davis's room. We could turf that patient if we needed the bed. Tonight, I don't think we will need to do much. You could already tell this was going to be a long night. We spent the first few hours cleaning or bathing the patients. It's never a nice thing if someone died and had not been bathed. Just seems wrong. After we gave the baths and any medications that the patients needed, we had to pull the arterial lines and arterial sheath out of two patients.

Dr. David Nash, one of our great cardiologists, always said, "pull the sheath out and let the first blood shoot out, then hold pressure. You can always guess at what someone's blood pressure is just by watching how far the blood will shoot."

We adopted that process, and it worked well. We often get nurses, especially new ones, coming into the unit to ask if they can practice pulling out the sheath under our supervision. One night, Deana came in and asked to pull the sheath out. "I need the practice, since we are going to pull them on the floor now." So, we went over the procedure, and she said she had it down.

Deana pulled on the sheath and the patient jumped. Sometimes the sheath does not come out smoothly. "Oh my god, what happened?" Well, we had blood all over the wall, but mostly it was on Deana. Her face was red not only from the blood, but from shock. Franco jumped in and stopped the bleeding until Deana regained her composure and wiped herself off. For us, it's kinda funny when this happens—but, not so funny for the patient. Tonight, all went well. There was no bleeding or mess to clean up.

By midnight, all was done—reports, charting, and tucking in the patients. Now, what to do for the next seven or so hours?

Kurt broke the silence; "Hey, I'm going on a break with Silvia."

"Okay." Katlin mumbled while she completed her charting. She didn't look up.

The Game

"I'm headed to the break room for coffee, anyone want one?" Palmer walked toward the break room. It was going to be one of those nights. Franco, Bev, and Barry wanted to play a board game. So, they started in on Monopoly. They all fought over who got the race car playing piece. Franco won, of course. I am not much for board games. Even as a kid living at home, I just could not get into them. Maybe that's why I took up cigars, jazz, and Scotch. They're my only vices. At least that is what I tell everyone. Usually, I will pour a Laphroaig or Highland Park (eighteen-year-old), light up a Cuban or CAO cigar, and turn the stereo on to John Coltrane, Sonny Rollins, Dizzy Gillespie, or Winton Marsalis. Once in a while, I chose to listen to the ladies of jazz—Diana Kroll, Natalie Cole, Norah Jones, Nina Simone. Sometimes, Fleetwood Mac was the best selection. I could go on and on.

The board game was well under way by the time I returned with my coffee and one for Katlin. Barry was complaining about being low on cash, and they had barely gone around the board a few times.

"Hey, Barry. I will loan you some money." Bev counted her money and laughed, "But you might owe me a favor later."

"Hey, Kurt. You back already? How's Silvia?" Barry deflected Bev's last comment.

"She's good, Barry. Ready for a break. She is getting burned out with the overtime shifts she has been picking up."

"Yeah, I hear you." Bev joined the conversation. "I'm ready for a break as well."

"Okay, people. Take five; let's check our patients before you get into that riveting game." Katlin now stood, getting ready to head into her rooms.

So, like little ducklings, we all went into our rooms to check on our patients. Good news, everyone was breathing. Like clockwork, we all came out of our rooms at the same time.

"Okay, back to the action." Barry was now energized. The three went back to their game. Kurt pulled out his book and began to read.

All seemed quiet around the hospital. A break for all the hard-working nurses. These are welcome shifts. It's easy to burn out if, day in and day out, it is crazy busy. These days or nights off set the bad ones. Katlin and I headed down to the ICSU. We wanted to stop in on ICU and say hi because we knew that Lisa, Pam, Thomas, and Holly were on tonight. They were another great crew, and they only had five patients, not bad. We keep tabs on each of the units as well as getting updates from the supervisors walking through.

"What's up, guys?" Tom walked over to Palmer so they could grasp each other's hand and give the customary bro hug.

"Not much. Looks as slow here as it is upstairs." Palmer surveyed the empty beds in ICU.

"Yeah, feels great." Thomas replied. "Hey, we on for golf this week?"

"Yeah, I can ask Barry and Franco. We should be able to get in a round or two."

The Game

"I'm ready to get out of here," Thomas continued. There's too much weird shit going on. Did you know they suspect a nurse is killing people in the hospital?"

"Is that what they think?" Katlin stepped in on the conversation.

"Who would do such a thing?" Holly joined in.

"Who knows why anyone does anything. We go to war, just because. They kill, just because; there is no reason, just actions and reactions." Holly added to the conversation.

"Holly that's getting too deep for me." Palmer laughed.

"Oh, shut up, Palmer." Holly laughed.

Thomas was in the Gulf War. Well, he was stationed in Germany and was due to deploy, but he never did get there. Thank God.

"Well, none-the-less, it just seems unreal to believe a thing like could happen." Holly watched as Lisa came over to the huddle.

"What are you talking about now? You guys play that stupid game, right? That seems wrong." Lisa was very hyper and fired a half dozen questions but never really waited for a response.

"How's Stephen, Lisa?" Katlin reached out to Lisa.

"Doing great. He is getting his energy back."

"You guys still playing your game, Katlin?" Lisa diverted the conversation.

"Well, it helps us learn and understand how the body functions, and how people react to different medications. Pharmacokinetics and pharmacodynamics play an important role in our work. We don't really set out to kill someone." Katlin defended what we do.

"Yeah, tell that to the person who is killing in this hospital. Many of these patients died mysteriously much like your game." Lisa seemed unaccountably hostile.

"Okay, which one of you did it?" Holly laughed, breaking the tension.

"Well, if you believe the rumor that a detective is looking at the staff, then yeah, I guess we are guilty." Katlin replied sarcastically. "Or, if you believe Martha, it's me."

"They have actually talked to us on a couple of occasions. There doesn't seem to be any real threat to us or any evidence." Silvia added to the conversation. "Just the fact that people see us walking around at nights, I guess that makes us guilty."

"Yeah, I think Martha and her team watch for all of us and have made a big deal out of it to the cops." Katlin smiled at the notion.

"Well, Katlin. We all go for walks. It's no big deal, but you are right. It seems to have become a big deal. The detective came in with Glover to talk to even us."

"So, what have the police been questioning you about?" Katlin looked more serious.

"Nothing worthwhile. They were asking what we knew about the deaths. If we saw anyone in the hallways or in the rooms where the deaths occurred, that sort of thing," Holly explained, jumping into the discussion.

"Ha! Ha! The detective asked if I killed anyone lately." Thomas added. "I laughed and said the night was not over, which was probably not the smartest reply. He asked if I was trying to be funny. I just replied 'no.'"

The Game

"Wow, Thomas! Are you crazy or something?" Silvia piped up.

"No, but I mentioned that when we run on codes, people die. You just never know if a person will survive or die."

All was silent, as we reflected on that.

"Well, let's hit the bricks." Katlin headed to the door.

"Okay, you guys. See you, and don't kill anyone tonight." Thomas laughed.

"You know, this is serious stuff." Katlin acted like a mom.

"Yeah, I get it., But if you can't laugh, you cry, or hold onto it until it makes you bitter."

"Hey, Kat. Let's head to ICSU."

"Sure, Palmer. You just want to see Diane, right?"

"Yeah."

Diane is a smart nurse who just happens to be a tall, pretty, Hispanic girl from Los Angeles. She was homecoming queen in high school. Diane had a hard time passing the nursing board. She knows her stuff, but she just doesn't take tests well. On the floor, she was great, treated her patients well and took good care of them. I helped her study when I worked on ICSU for a short time. She taught me Spanish, and, in turn, I tutored her in nursing. She passed the boards, and I learned how to swear in Spanish.

Diane and I had a short thing going during the study sessions. I often went over and ended up staying the night. Diane lived with a roommate who was never around much. This gave Diane and me a chance to relax. Things started slow—talks, then back messages and the odd shower after we worked out at the gym, finally intimacy. I think many girls are jealous or envious of Diane. Like I said, she is twenty-something with raven-black hair, brown eyes, and about 5 feet 10 inches tall. She could have easily been a model. Many people were glad to see her struggle with the exams. But Diane is a great person; she's very sincere and hardworking. Her family did not have much money and said if she wanted to go to school, she would have to pay for it. So, she worked to put herself through nursing school. Diane did and does live in an apartment with a roommate. She has a boyfriend who was in Arizona. I'm not sure if or when he is coming back. He never made it back for months at a time, leaving a very lonely Diane.

"Hola cómo estás, Diane?"

"Hey, Palmer, Katlin. What's going on? What brings you to ICSU Hell?" Diane greeted them, including the affectionate name for ICSU.

"Not much, just out for a walk." Katlin sounded a little put off.

"It's been busy with all the people coming through here." Diane motioned down the hall. "First, Tara came and left; then Victor came and left. Not sure why we need two RTs tonight; we are slow. But I guess we will take what we get."

"Oh, that does seem odd." Katlin perked up a little.

"Yeah." Diane started to rationalize why both RTs had gone into the same rooms. "Perhaps one started the treatment, and the other finished it."

"Perhaps," Katlin thought out loud. "So, Tara is your assigned RT tonight?"

"No, Victor is on our call list."

Each floor gets a call list that includes the names of supervisors, the MD on call, an RT, the transplant team, and

The Game

others. Usually, it's accurate. Occasionally, someone might call in or have extra, and the list does not always get updated.

"Well, let's roll Mr. It's time to get back before Kurt comes looking for us, or someone gets the wrong idea."

"Adiós, Di. Mantente caliente."

"What?"

"I mean, mantente fresco."

"Always, you too, boss." Diane nicknamed me *boss* when I tutored her. I was trying to be funny, during one of our sessions and told her that she had to call me boss while I was her teacher. So, she did and has never stopped.

"Want to get a drink sometime, boss?"

"Sure, Di. That would be nice."

"Okay, it's a date."

"Well, what's that about boss?" Katlin smiled at the nickname.

"Skeletons in the closet, Katlin."

"Oh, so I'm not the only one?" Katlin was still making fun of Palmer.

"Sorry, is that wrong?"

"No, we have what we have, no commitments. I'm just messing with you."

Back on the home front, Kurt was still reading. The book must have been good. Barry was out of the Monopoly game and in debt to Bev. It looked like Franco had stockpiled all the hotels and houses, while Bev was staying afloat.

"Oh my god. Will this night never end?" Barry paced around the unit.

"Not soon enough." Kurt stated without looking up from his book.

"How're the kids? Katlin referred to the patients.

"All is good, boss," Damien responded from the monitoring station. Damien is our eyes on almost all the critical care patients who need telemetry. His sole job is to do that and let us know if someone is having arrhythmia problems.

Bang! The doors bust out. "What's up, gringos?" Victor stood there, smiling.

"Hey, quiet. I'm about to win all the money." Franco laughed like a mad scientist. Bev gave him the stare of disgust.

"What you doin'?" Barry acted all gangster.

"Not much, man; just doing my rounds."

"Hey, Victor! You and Tara tag teaming tonight?" Katlin jumped into the conversation.

"No, why you asking?"

"No reason. ICSU said they saw the two of you on the unit."

"Oh, yeah. Well, we are sharing the work tonight. There's not much going on."

"Uh! Makes sense." Katlin sat back down.

"Well, I'm outa here, gringos. Gotta keep an eye on the old lady." Victor headed to the doors.

"Alright! Take it easy, Victor!" Barry walked toward Victor as he leaves.

"Hey, its 3:00 a.m.; time for vital signs, yeahaaa!!!"

Bev jumped up from her seat. So, we all got up and checked our patients. Usually we plan to check the patients on the hour; some do require constant checks,

"All is well." Franco strolled out of his room.

"Yep, same." Bev replied, almost disappointed.

"Palmer, wait up. I have a question for you." Katlin motioned for me to come over. I took my time getting to the room.

"What's up, Kat? I need to check my patients now that we are back."

"Call me crazy, but do you think Victor could be the guy behind these killings?"

"No way, why? What's his motive?"

"Yeah, you may be right. But it seems odd that he and Tara are doing rounds together. They never round together."

"True, but, as Di said, it's slow, and we are all looking for something to do."

"Okay, Palmer, if you say so. It just seems odd. I guess this thing about Mary steams me. I want to understand the motive behind her death and the others. I just can't imagine what is happening."

"Kurt, want to go for a walk with me?" Bev asked, like a school girl.

"Sure, Bev. We hardly go for walks anymore."

"What did I say!? I can't help you if you continue to do this. It's wrong no matter what the hospital admin is doing."

"Well, it's not fair, and I want to see them pay."

"How!? How does this help?"

"Because the hospital won't get reaccredited. That's how! If they lose accreditation, they lose money, and people will get fired. Then, maybe, they will listen and

pay people what is coming to them, and you will get what you deserve."

"Okay, let's talk later. Let's get out of here."

Bev walked toward the dark hallway on the fifth floor with a purpose.

"Kurt, let's head down to ICSU. I want to chat with the crew." Marching on, Bev and Kurt headed down to ICSU. Just as they turned the corner to ICSU, they nearly ran into Victor and Tara.

"H! How you doing, Tara?" Bev exclaimed, clearly excited to see her. "What's up, girl? How have you been?"

"Doing well, I haven't seen you much up on the seventh floor." Bev leaned in for a hug.

"No, I've been trying to focus on the middle floors. There have been lots of interesting pulmonary concerns down here." Tara reciprocated the hug.

"Hey, were you guys just on fifth?" Bev looked at her friend.

"Tara, we gotta run. We have a couple treatments to do." Victor motioned to Tara.

"Oh, okay, Victor. Yeah, gotta run, girl. Take it easy. Let's get together soon."

"You bet, let's go for drinks." Bev used her thumb and pinky finger like a phone.

"Kurt, let's get back to the unit, unless you want to say hi to Silvia while we are here. Or, you can take me on the stairwell." Bev grinned.

"No, I'm good. Let's go. You ask me this every time, and each time I say no. What would Silvia say?" Kurt let the invite slide.

One thing for sure is, you never know if Bev was real or all pretend. At work, she is all business, but outside of the workplace, she is different. She cuts loose.

"Well, it's about time you two got back. Franco acted like a concerned dad. How was your date?"

"Sorry. We stopped in the stairwell for a quickie." Bev snapped back, and Kurt just grinned.

CODE BLUE 6F, CODE BLUE 6F the alarm breaks the silence of the night.

"My turn." Katlin belted out as she grabbed the lifepak and headed out the door.

"What the hell did you do?! I thought I made it clear?"

"No, I said it's a means to an end."

"Go now. Before people see us both. I will work this."

Dr. Sandoval arrived quickly, most likely because the ER was not busy. Katlin arrived next, and she connected the patient to the monitor and printed out a rhythm strip. Next, Holly arrived from ICU. Victor arrived to get things ready respiratory-wise. Okay, what's up! Dr. Sandoval asked. The floor nurse looked a little dazed and confused. It seems whenever we go on codes, the floor nurse needs a second to regroup. I think they just do not expect something like this to happen.

Nancy finally piped up, "Well, I'm not sure. One minute she was fine and the next she was gagging and couldn't breathe."

"Okay, let's intubate her and send her to ICU. She looks swollen, as if she was having an allergic reaction."

"Holly, do you have room?"

"Yep. Let me call Lisa to give her a heads-up."

"Victor, bag her, and let's drop a tube."

"Got it, doc. I'm ready when you are."

Dr. Sandoval intubated, and Victor continued to bag the patient with 100 percent oxygen. Holly started a line just to be sure.

"Okay, it looks like she is stable, just not breathing. Could be that she is allergic to something." Sandoval spoke to everyone.

"Only peanuts," Nancy replied.

"But how would she be exposed to nuts at 3:30 a.m.?"

"Well, with that type of allergy, you never know. Someone could have had peanut dust on their hands and touched something the patient touched."

Holly, Victor, and the floor nurse transported the patient down to ICU and got her settled. Holly gave the patient some valium to relax her and let the patient sleep now that she has been intubated. Reports given, and the final transfers were complete. Holly takes vital signs, while getting the patient tucked in.

After we run on a code, most of us need to replay what we did. We ask ourselves and each other questions, like 'Could there have been something else we should have done?' While

The Game

questioning our actions might seem as if we lack professional confidence, it is actually good to do this because it allows us to learn from the present actions and the past.

"Palmer, come over here. I need to speak to you."

"Sure, Kat. How was the code?" Palmer walked over casually.

"It was an anaphylactic reaction due to a peanut allergy. She was intubated and sent to ICU."

"Wow, that's lucky."

"Yeah, but I saw something……"

"Oh, do tell." Palmer now perked up.

"Well, I was coming to the room and saw Tara leaving quickly."

"She probably had something going on."

"Well, yeah. But I saw peanut shells, like the ones from Logan's. It looked like Tara had dropped them. It was dark, so I was not sure."

"So, you think Tara had peanuts on her hands and caused this?"

"Well, yes. But I am also thinking that she and Victor might be the people killing our patients."

"Well, they do have access. But why would they do such a thing?"

"Not sure, Palmer. But if that's the case, they are both are still out there and headed back to ICU."

Palmer looked around to make sure no one is in earshot.

"Stop fucking around!! I don't want any more shit happening, got it?!

"Hey, sometimes you gotta step in shit to get what you want. Don't you want what I want?"

"Yeah! But not like this."

"Tara, you need to get out of here while I think of something."

Usually the nurse who runs on the code takes the patient. Mostly because they know what went on. So, Holly will take this patient and give up her other patient. This is a standard because the patient could easily go south, and we'd have to code her again. The first few hours are critical.

The patient was still awake and restless.

"Ms. Hendricks, relax. We have you in ICU now. The tube is to help you breathe." The patient was still motioning about something, but Holly was unable to make out what she wanted.

The Game

FOUR A.M.

It's time to turn the patients, do vital signs, and make sure all tubes are attached and functioning. That's our usual 4:00 a.m. protocol. Everyone is alive and comfortable. It's during this time of the shift that many codes are called and deaths are found. The floors do vital signs only at midnight and 4:00 a.m. One particular night, we had a code blue on the orthopedic floor. We all arrived to the room to see the patient sitting up in his bed. Only problem was, he was dead. The floor nurse said when she walked by the room, she saw him sitting up and just assumed he was good. So, at 4:00 a.m. she went in to say hi and found him dead. We went to lay him back in the bed. He was so stiff that he was lying in bed with his legs curled up, just like he was sitting. The patient died in his sleep.

"Okay, okay, calm down, Mrs. Hendricks. Let the machine do the breathing for you. Wait, I can't understand what you want."

Holly, very frustrated with her patient's actions, gave her some more valium to relax her.

Often, people fight the endotracheal tube (ET) and think they can't breathe, so we have to sedate them and slowly wean them off the vent.

"'Hi, Holly.'" Lisa stepped into the room, "How is the patient doing?"

"Okay, I guess. She seems like she is fighting the tube a little, so I gave her something to relax with. But, after the two doses of solumedrol, the swelling is down; she looks much better."

"Okay, let's try to get her ready for the day shift. We can clean some of these patients out for the week."

"Okay Lis, I will. I'll say one thing; it almost looked like Ms. Hendricks was afraid of something."

'Oh, like what? You know she will be afraid. This is a new bed and strange place.'

"Well, I'm not sure. But it seemed like she was afraid of Victor. She was pointing at him with crazy eyes."

"It's so hard to say. She could have recognized him from upstairs and just wanted the tube out."

"You're probably right, Lis. That's why you get paid the big bucks." Holly laughed and got back to work on Ms. Hendricks. It was not long before the patient was awake, calm, and following directions from Holly.

"I'm going to call RT and have them check the pulmonary pressures, and, hopefully, we'll get the tube out, Ms. Hendricks."

The patient nodded her head in agreement.

"Okay, Ms. Hendricks, I called RT, and someone will be coming shortly."

We take things slow with patients on ventilators. We want them to do most of the work when it comes to breathing. After they start to relax and breathe, we can begin to wean the vent down and eventually pull the tube out.

Lis left Holly to get things set up in the room for RT. Because the respiratory department have only a few people, we try to get as much ready as possible. This allows the technician to come in, check pulmonary pressures, extubate, and get out.

"Hola, qué tal, gringas?"

The Game

"Holly, Victor is here." laughing at his entrance, Lisa showed Victor into the room.

"Hey, chicas! Oh, you too, Thomas" Victor laughed while coughing at the same time.

Victor and Thomas have been good friends for some time. Both were in the war in the Middle East. Victor saw more action than Thomas did and reminds him whenever he gets the chance. It was during this tour that Victor said he came into contact with some sort of toxic gas that caused his respiratory problems. Victor went from one doctor to another to get a diagnosis, but no one would go on the record that the pulmonary problems came from the war.

"Funny, Victor, real funny'"

"Victor, let's try to get that tube out of Ms. Hendricks, so we can transfer her in the morning," Lisa instructed Victor.

"See what we can do, Ms. Boss lady"

'Hi, Holly! You got my stuff ready?"

"Yeah, let's do this." Holly replied.

Victor has to provide instructions to the patient, to see if they can follow directions. Pulmonary function tests (PFTs) are a group of tests that measure how well your lungs work. This includes how well you're able to breathe and how effective your lungs are able to bring oxygen to the rest of your body. To remove the ventilator, the respiratory technician will perform variations of this test.

"Okay, Ms. Hendricks, I want you to take a couple deep breaths, as big as you can. Then, I will put you back on the vent and let you catch your breath."

Ms. Hendricks nodded her understanding.

"Okay, ready? Go—deep, deep breath, big, big, big. Okay, good work. Catch your breath." Victor placed the patient back on the vent to allow her to catch her breath. "Okay. Now, you can take a deep breath and blow it all out, like candles on a cake, Ms. Hendricks. Ready? Deep breath, ready, and blow, blow, blow, go, go, go. Good. Okay, catch your breath and we will be back in one minute."

"I think she is ready, right, Victor?"

Holly got a few things ready to pull the tube out. Usually, we need suction, a 10-cc syringe to remove the air from the ET balloon, and some towels to catch the tube.

"Well, she is close, Holly. We may be able to remove the tube."

"Hey, Victor. I need to speak to you." Tara poked her head into the room.

"Oh, hey Tara." Holly acknowledged her.

"Okay, let me pull this tube, and I'll be right there'"

"No, I need you now. It's important."

Just as Tara and Victor started to talk, the alarms sounded on the vent. Ms. Hendricks was coughing and her blood pressure was sky high. At that moment, Ms. Hendricks was also sitting upright and pointing frantically toward the door.

"Yes, Ms. Hendricks, you will be able to leave once the tube is out. Please, lay back down, Holly tried to restrain her patient." But Ms. Hendricks is now resisting Holly and gesturing wildly at the door.

"Victor! Now!" Tara stalked away from the door.

"What is going on, babe? Victor leaned into Tara.

The CCU staff are sitting around the table. Some are charting; others are just relaxing.

The Game

"Bev, I think I know what is happening." Katlin looked anxious.

"What do you mean, with the deaths, is that what you are saying?" Bev was standing close to Katlin as they talked.

"Katlin, what is it? Franco questioned, overhearing the conversation.

"Franco, I think something is going on with Victor. He seems jumpy and evasive."

"I need to call ICU!" Katlin reached for the phone while the rest of the crew are staring at her with blank or confused looks.

It was at this same time the ICU phone rang.

"ICU. Lisa speaking."

"Lisa, this is Katlin, I..."

"Hi, Katlin. Your patient is doing okay, but the alarms are going crazy. Wait one second. I'll be back." Lisa interrupted Katlin.

Lisa runs over to the room to see what the commotion is about.

"Holly, what's up?"

"I'm not sure Lis, she is very excited and will not relax and lay back."

"Okay, you girls calm her down. Tara and I will be right back." Victor strolled out the door.

"I think we need to sedate her, Holly." Lis pointed to the syringe of valium.

Ms. Hendricks is shaking her head side-to-side, saying no. She takes a few breaths, like Victor showed her, and she relaxes back, but she motions for the tube to be pulled out.

"We can't pull the tube just yet. Please relax." Holly tried to comfort the patient.

Ms. Hendricks writes something in the air.

"What is it, Ms. Hendricks." Holly is now very emotional.

"Lisa, get her some paper, and let's see what she wants."

"Okay, be right back." Lisa ran to the desk.

"Okay, Ms. Hendricks. We will get you some paper, so you can communicate to us until the respiratory technician returns."

Lisa returned with paper and pen.

"Here you go." Holly gave the paper and pen to Ms. Hendricks.

"Okay, Ms. Hendricks. Please tell us what you want." Holly looking down at Ms. Hendricks franticly writing.

"KILL….Kill me!!"

"Oh, no, Ms. Hendricks. We are not trying to kill you, we are helping." Holly replied.

Ms. Hendricks shook her head again… NO

"Her…Kill…me…Peanuts…"

"Please, sit back, Ms. Hendricks. Let me talk to Lisa, she is in charge tonight. I will be right back." Lisa and Holly stepped out to the doorway.

Ms. Hendricks nodded in agreement.

"Lisa, oh my god, look!"

"Holly, what did she write?" Lisa looked down at the paper.

'Well this," Holly showed the paper to Lisa.

"Oh, my god!! Is this true?" Lisa picked up the phone.

"Hello, hey Katlin. Sorry, I forgot you were on the line. I can't talk. I have a situation."

The Game

"Lisa, I know. I think I know…"

"Talk soon. Bye, Katlin."

"Damn it, she hung up on me." Katlin cursed.

"Hey watch our patients; guys. I need to run to ICU to warn Lisa. Palmer come with me."

Katlin practically ran out the door with Palmer in hot pursuit.

"Sure, Katlin. Bev volunteered. I'll watch. You guys go make out… I mean run to ICU." Bev laughed, still with one thing on her mind, as the two sped out the door.

"We need to get to ICU. Something is up, Palmer."

"Sure, Kat. Let's go."

"Are you crazy? Why did you come down to ICU, Tara?"

"I needed to warn you that she saw me, Victor."

"No shit. Now she has the attention of the unit. You should leave, now"

"I can't, where would I go?' Besides, I need to be with you."

"Tara, this is so messed up. I am not sure I can help. If you run, you might have a chance. If you stay, they will arrest you."

"But, Victor, this is not the way I had it planned. I wanted the hospital and those bureaucrats to suffer. With all these deaths, the feds would pull funding,

and the feds would see that you are the one in need, and that they should give you the benefits you deserve. They need to understand that our war vets are the ones we should take care of. You fought for us all. You were exposed to some toxic shit that messed your breathing up, that's not right. Someone needs to be accountable and take care of you and others like you."

"But, I'm not sure this was the answer, Tara."

"Maybe not, but it is the only way to get people to listen."

"You must go. I will stall them. Good-bye, my dear. I love you."

"I love you, Victor. I always will."

"Victor, someone is over there, at the end of the hall."

"Okay, go! I will see who it is."

"Hey, Victor! What's up?" Katlin questioned shakily. Their rapid descent had winded her slightly, but she was also convinced that a killer was in front of her.

"Oh, hey Katlin, Palmer. What brings you out at this time?" Victor looked a little flushed and sweaty.

"It's slow upstairs, so we came for a walk." Katlin tried to come up with an excuse to be on the fourth floor.

"Was that, Tara?" Palmer interrupted.

"No, that was, uh, Megan. She wanted to know where the extra oxygen tanks are."

The Game

"Oh, it looked like you were standing pretty close to her, like it was Tara."

"Well, what can I say?"

"Not much." Katlin stepped in, "what would Tara say?"

"Yeah, you're right. Let's not say anything to her." Victor laughed nervously.

"Well, gotta run, amigos." Victor wheezed heavily.

"Wait, Victor. There's something going on."

"Boy, for a slow night, he was in a big hurry, wasn't he?" Katlin said as they sprinted toward ICU.

"Yeah, seems odd for him. But then again, it's a full moon, and strange stuff happens."

"I wonder if he is running away, or going to find Tara?"

"Possible. Should we follow him, Kat?"

"No, we can call Smith from ICU."

Katlin and I continued sprinting to ICU, through the dark hall "Hey you, whatz up?" Diane stepped out of her room. "You come back to confirm our date, Palmer?"

"Have you seen Victor or Tara? They were supposed to do a treatment on 448 B".

"Yeah, we just saw him. Maybe he's on his way; he was in a big rush. But, he was headed in the opposite direction." Palmer replied, a little short of breath.

"No matter, I got Megan to do it."

"Wait, what? Megan was just back down the hall." Palmer stopped suddenly.

"She moves fast." Palmer tried to remember if he had seen anyone pass by them.

"No, she has been here for ten minutes. Why do you say that?" Diane walked out into the hallway now.

"Well, Victor and Megan were just talking at the other end of the unit about extra oxygen tanks."

"No, must have been someone else. She has been here with me," Diane pointed into the room.

"Okay, well, whatever. Palmer added. We just wanted to say hi to ICU before the shift ends." Palmer didn't want to give any details.

"Okay, is all okay? You seem to be in a rush."

"No, we are good; nothing's going on." Palmer caught up to Katlin.

"Okay, you coming to the gym after work, Palmer? I can meet you there."

"Sure, I am ready for a workout. But, let me call you to confirm before we leave."

"No problem, Palmer. I am going, no matter what. I need a good workout."

Palmer and Katlin speed walk toward ICU. Just as they arrive, Glover appears.

"Hi guys." Mr. Glover walks up to Katlin and Palmer as Palmer opens the door to ICU.

"Hey, Richard. What's going on?" Katlin asked. "I think we need Smith, I think I know who the killer is!"

"Have you seen Victor or Tara? I need to talk to them."

"Yeah, Victor was just down the hall a few minutes ago. Not sure where Tara is. We need to find them. They are the ones." Katlin was breathing heavily from the sprint down the hall.

"Okay, thanks." Mr. Glover headed back down the hall. "I'll make the call!"

The Game

"Yes, find Tara and Victor, they need to explain, I'm headed in to let Lis know what's going on."

"Call or page me if you see them, ASAP! I'll call Smith." Glover barking orders.

"Everyone is in a rush, I think we are right. Tara and Victor are up to something." Katlin looked at Palmer and rushed into the unit to talk to Lisa.

"Lisa, Is our patient okay?" Katlin looked into the room over Lisa's shoulder.

"Yeah, look what she wrote! I called Glover the supervisor. Ms. Hendricks thinks someone is trying to kill her."

"Wow, Lisa! That's what I wanted to talk to you about. I saw Tara coming out of the room in a hurry. She looked like she was dropping peanut shells or something."

"Peanuts. So, did she cause the reaction in Ms. Hendricks?"

"Well, I noticed she had peanuts in her hands. So yes, that probably was the cause of Ms. Hendricks anaphylactic reaction."

"Yeah, turns out Tara gave her some peanut powder, which sent her into anaphylactic shock." Palmer added his comments. Katlin saw her, and we put two and two together."

"What? No way. That's not Tara. Why would she do such a thing?" Lisa still can't believe what is transpiring.

"Yeah, she might have been the one who killed a few others. Glover is calling the police now."

"Glover and the police need to get here. I'm sure they will need to question those two." Palmer commented.

"Oh, my god! We just spoke to Victor about ten minutes ago. That must have been Tara who was with him when we interrupted their conversation. But we could not see the girl. Victor said it was Megan, but turns out Megan was on ICSU."

"Did you tell Mr. Glover?" Lisa talked faster now.

"Yes, but only briefly. He ran to make the call." Katlin's heart was racing.

The doors crash open and Glover and Smith burst through the door.

"Mr. Smith!" Katlin saw him coming through the doors.

"Thank god you're here. It's Victor and Tara. We need to find them." Lisa pointed out the doors.

"Yes, Glover called to let us know that the killers are in the hospital."

"We saw Victor and probably Tara just a few minutes ago, but they both left quickly." Katlin was almost breathless.

"No worries, we have men around the hospital and at their house. We will get them. Glover said it could be these two, so we had black and whites go to their house and are covering the hospital doors."

"Do you really believe they killed others?" Palmer reacted to Smith.

"Once we apprehend them and question them, we will know."

"Oh, my god. So, she was killing people. But why? Lisa asked the big question.

"We will find that out soon." Smith reached for his radio and spoke into it. "Anything yet?"

"We got them both. They were leaving out the back door, and we have them in custody now."

"Hold them, I will be there shorty. Glover, take me to the back doors."

"Right, this way, Smith." Both rushed back out the doors.

"Oh my god, did we just catch a murderer?" Katlin took a deep breath.

"Katlin, that was so good of you and Palmer." Lis flopped down on a chair.

"I'm going to call the unit, Kat. Let them know what's going on."

"Yes, make sure all is okay up there."

> "I knew you were bitter and wanted justice from the government and the hospital. Victor, you are miserable and wanted some sort of restitution. However, none came, no matter who we talked to. I wanted to make it right. Show everyone you're the victim.
>
> "But you took it way too far, Tara. Yes, I wanted revenge on the corporate structure but not like this. I would never harm someone to gain monetarily. I love you and no way could I stand by and watch what happens to you, Tara. I first discovered the crimes when I ran in on a patient who needed a nebulization treatment, but I was late getting to the patient. When I arrived, I found you administering a medication. But it was not the prescribed albuterol. It was a white, powdered substance. So, I called the code, to try to save the patient, and you. What the hell have you done, Tara?"
>
> "Victor, I did it for you? I cannot stand what they have done to you. You were alive and vibrant. But

now, now you are just here, barely any life left in you. I killed these people to send this hospital a message. Without their precious little accreditation, this hospital would have to listen and promote the good people like you. You are the brains behind many of our policies, but it's Kerry who takes all the credit. She stole your position, your deserved position."

"But, baby, not like this. What is it worth if we need to run? Our lives will never be the same, no matter what happens."

"But it is, I covered our tracks and put the blame on those two smart-alecky nurses. No one suspects me."

"I did. I suspected you were doing something like this. So, if I know, it will not be long before others figure this out. I've tried to cover your tracks. By doing so, people suspect me."

"I was careful; they suspect someone else."

"Yes, but they all suspect me, and now, you. I saw Glover nosing around. So, you need to run."

"But where will I go without you?"

"Okay, let's both go now."

"Freeze, police! Don't move you are both under arrest." Tara and Victor were instantly surrounded by the police.

"We got them both, they were leaving out the back door and we have them in custody now."

"Hold them, I will be there shorty." Smith on the other end of the radio.

Smith and Glover running down to the back doors.

"Hey, Glover. We have a couple black and whites that will drive them downtown. I will need to finish up some work. Tell Katlin, thanks."

"Thanks, detective. I will let the nurses know."

FINAl CHAPTER

Just as Smith stated, the hospital was surrounded with police. Tara and Victor tried to leave through the back doors that only the staff know about. But when they headed to their car, they were spotted. Both Tara and Victor gave up without any hassle.

Mr. Glover headed to ICU to let them know that all was clear and that both Tara and Victor had been arrested.

"Thanks, Richard, for letting us know. Ms. Hendricks is good now, and she's safe."

Glover also headed up to CCU to let the team know the situation. Everyone was safe, and things could now return to normal.

The shift ended and reports were given to the day staff. It was only a matter of minutes until the story spread to all the units and floors in the hospital.

Martha is on days today....

"Hey, drinks on me at Logan's." Katlin motioned to the door.

"Do you know where it is? Franco laughed as we all left. Franco had never thought that Katlin went out much.

"I have GPS, Franco. I'll find it"

LOGAN'S ROADHOUSE

"So, whatever led Tara to kill people for Victor?" Franco sat down with his two beers in hand.

Jerry carried a Scotch and a whiskey over to Katlin and me. "Here, mate, on the house. Cheers."

"Thanks, Jerry." Palmer looked very surprised.

"Yeah, don't piss off, Kat, or I will stab you, mate." Jerry stated with a half-smile and looked at the others.

"Who knows," Kurt grabbed at his beer. "I guess if you love someone enough, you'll do anything."

"Wow, would you kill for Silvia?" Barry asked between sips of beer.

"Maybe, I'm not sure." Kurt thought about the situation. "Let me think about that."

"What? You would not kill anyone for me?" Silvia looked at Kurt in a disapproving, but loving manner.

"So, Tara took our game and turned it into real life." Bev leaned back in her chair, stretching and pushing her boobs out even farther than they already reached.

"Well, she and Victor were in and out of the unit all the time. They must have overheard our plans in the game." Palmer sipped his MacCallum eighteen-year-old Scotch.

"If it wasn't for Mrs. Hendricks, I mean if she had died, Tara would still be free. Tara was a good friend of mine. I would have never guessed she could do such a heinous act." Bev sipped on her Crown and Coke.

"You know this place is full of peanut dust and shells. Do you think Tara grabbed dust from here and gave it to that patient?" Barry asked and looked a little nervous.

The Game

"What happens to Victor?" Silvia asked as she reached for Kurt's hand.

"He goes to jail for conspiracy to commit murder." Mr. Smith now stood over the group like a high school principal.

"We suspected a few people, but had no real leads. If Tara didn't overhear you game, most likely Victor would have and talked to Tara about it."

"So, you came after me." Katlin ignored the remarks and sat forward.

"Well, yes. Glad it turned out for you and the team, Katlin. You helped us out with your digging into your friend's death. I just wanted to fill you in on a few things"

"Thanks." Katlin moved a chair over.

"Care to join us, Mr. Smith?" Bev pulled the chair closer to her.

"Game over for both," Franco looked at his half-empty second beer.

"So, as you know Victor is sick. He has asthma and some other medical problems that you probably know better than me."

"I'll say, Barry stepped in. He always complained about his illness. How it was the government's fault. Then, once at the hospital, he complained because they gave him no benefits for a pre-existing disease."

"Right, so it was because of this Tara wanted to get back at the hospital administration. She explained to us that if the hospital lost their accreditation, the hospital would be in jeopardy of losing millions of dollars."

"How does that help Victor, Mr. Smith?" Bev eyed the slightly older man sitting close to her.

"Tara explained to us during our questioning that if the hospital lost millions and the accreditation that that would force administration to look hard at the standard operating procedures and how they bill for services. Plus, she thought the administration would all be canned and a new administration would review these polices and help their workers. Smith motioned to the bar tender for some water.

"So, Victor was in on it, right detective?" Kurt leaned on his elbows now.

"Actually, no. He said he really tried to stop her. He was late coming in on the first patient who died. He thought if he could save the patient, he could save Tara." Smith took the water from Jerry. "Thank you." The problem is that he knew right from the beginning. So that makes him an accessory to the fact. He will serve time, as will Tara. One can rationalize actions to make them fit any situation. We see this every day in the news. People killing and blowing things up in the name of a god or a religion. People see a wrong and insist that it be made right. When letters and protests don't work, the only alternative is action. It is that action that can cross a line. Is it right to kill to be heard? The means do not justify the end. Tara believed the only reasonable action was to take lives to get the attention of the administration or establishment. If she could affect the hospital's bottom line, perhaps changes would occur. She thought they would learn to understand that people, all people need to be treated fairly and honestly, with respect and dignity. Tara believed Victor was placed in harm's way when the government tested biological agents, and good people were killed or became sick. The government did not take responsibility for their actions, so Tara believed they needed to pay. When the hospital chose not to honor their agreement to care for people like Victor and others like him, the administration needed to be punished. If the administrators lost financing, she felt that perhaps policies would change. Collateral damage was the only means to an end, so thought Tara. If enough people became enraged, policies might change. Killing patients was that collateral damage."

"Wow! That's quite the speech, Detective Smith." Katlin looked over at Smith.

"Well, that was Tara's statement, not my words."

"Did she say why she killed Mary? Mary had nothing to do with this hospital." Katlin became a little more upset than she wanted.

"Well, actually she did. She was hoping to enrage you to take action against administration, but instead you channeled your anger into her chart and found those changes Tara had created. She thought this was when we, or rather you knew something was horribly wrong."

"Yes, there was not much to go on before that. I know Dr. Brooks had some ideas, but certainly could not identify a killer. Katlin relaxed a little now.

"Detective, let me buy to a drink. You can stay and chat with me… ah us." Bev placed an arm around Smith's arm.

"No, I have to get back to the office and write this up. I also have other work to do. New case over at some pharmaceutical research facility."

ANOTHER WEEK

CODE BLUE, 6E, CODE BLUE 6E

"Barry… Don't kick the door…."

"One of these days, I will smack that kid!" Bev shouted, as Barry ran down the halls.

The End

ACKNOWLEDGEMENTS

Thanks to Christoph Koniczek at Friesen Press for making me believe that I am a writer and I have something to contribute.

I want to give a special thanks to my editor Joyce. We talked and discussed the characters, the plot, and the structure of this book on several occasions. Thank you for your amazing comments and support throughout this process.

Thank you to the entire team at Friesen Press. It truly was a team effort to get the book completed and published. From conception to completion. Thank you all.

Printed in Canada